the love of a bad man

Laura Elizabeth Woollett is a Perth-born, Melbourne-based author and editor. Her first novel, *The Wood of Suicides*, was published in the US in early 2014. From 2012 to early 2015 she was a fiction editor for *Voiceworks*. More recently, she appeared as one of Melbourne Writers Festival's '30 Under 30'. Her work has appeared widely in print and online, including in *Kill Your Darlings*, *The Suburban Review*, and *Literary Hub*.

the love of a bad man

LAURA ELIZABETH WOOLLETT

SCRIBE
Melbourne • London

Scribe Publications
18–20 Edward St, Brunswick, Victoria 3056, Australia
2 John St, Clerkenwell, London, WC1N 2ES, United Kingdom

First published by Scribe 2016

These stories first appeared in the following publications: 'Caril' and 'Karla' (as 'Sweetheart Deal') in *Voiceworks*; 'Charlie's Girls' in *The Suburban Review*; 'Wanda' in *Skidrow Penthouse*; 'Eva' (excerpt) on The Wheeler Centre website.

Typeset in 12/17 pt Adobe Garamond Pro by the publisher

Printed and bound in the UK by CPI Group (UK) Ltd, Croydon, CR0 4YY

Scribe Publications is committed to the sustainable use of natural resources and the use of paper products made responsibly from those resources.

CiP data records for this title are available from the National Library of Australia and the British Library.

9781925321555 (Australian edition)
9781911344247 (UK edition)
9781925307788 (e-book)

scribepublications.com.au
scribepublications.co.uk

CONTENTS

What hills, what hills are those, my love

Those hills so dark and low?

Those are the hills of hell, my love

Where you and I must go.

'THE DAEMON LOVER', CHILD BALLAD 243

Blanche

'Baby, wake up,' he says, and he's kissing my eyelids, my cheeks, trailing his fingers over the bib of my nightgown and it's so soft it must be a dream. Buck home. Buck home after fifteen months. But the telegram was only this afternoon and his bus won't be getting to Dallas till morning and there's the long dusty drive after that. It's night now. The room is dark and from the window I can feel a cool wind blowing in, bringing smells of flowering pecan and hackberry. Buck kisses me again.

'Wake up, baby,' he says.

'Daddy?' My voice sounds strange and syrupy-thick. I've been fixing to make him a big breakfast since I heard he was getting out, flapjacks and bacon all drowning in sweetness the way he likes. 'Is this real, or am I dreaming?'

Buck laughs and I feel his ribs shaking under my hands. After all his time inside, they're jutting something awful. That's how I know he's really here, and also because he's touching me, putting his hands all up my nightgown. He kisses me on the lips, so sweet and long and glad it makes my cheeks hurt.

'Daddy …' I try to say. He smooches my mouth corner. 'Daddy, how'd you get here so fast?'

The trunk is packed and I'm wearing a new outfit, white-and-gold check with fresh white gloves and white pumps to match. Buck lets out a low whistle when I come down the porch, holding my straw hat to my head.

'I've got me a little yellow songbird,' he booms out to his ma and sister, both standing with crossed arms under the pecan tree. They don't laugh or even hardly smile. I know they think me vain for putting money into my appearance in hard times like this, but I'll be darned if I don't look my best for Buck his first day of freedom.

'You come back soon as you can, son,' his ma hugs him tight and pushes her cheek up against his. 'You hear me?'

'Aw, Ma, you know me and Blanche wanna get settled right away.'

But Mrs Barrow won't take no for an answer, and soon he's stroking her hair, telling her we'll be back in a week or two at the latest. Then he kisses Marie goodbye and I do the same to his ma, thanking her for her hospitality. 'It's nothing,' she says, but I feel her cheek stiffen under my lips and know she's only saying it for Buck's benefit. The truth is, his people have never made me feel too welcome. I guess they can't forgive me for being the most important person in his life.

'Let's shake some dust, baby,' Buck winks at me over Marie's head.

Dirt flies up as we pull away from the house and I wave at them through the pale storm of it. I don't know what sight makes me happier: Mrs Barrow and Marie getting smaller behind us, or the big blue sky ahead of us.

As we drive through town, Buck puts his hand on my knee. He laughs to himself. 'What's funny?' I ask him. He just shakes his head and laughs some more. Well, I don't like him making a game of me, so I keep asking, 'What's funny, Daddy?' until he squeezes my knee and shakes his head again. Then he whistles.

'I'm a free man. Oh, lordy. I'm a free man.'

We're just passing through town when I pull out my compact. Buck jokes that it's going to be hard getting used to all my lotions and potions again. I've been working at the Cinderella Beauty Shoppe these past months, so I know a thing or two about makeup, but for once I don't have anything to say about it. The reason being, I've just caught sight of the black Oldsmobile that's tailing us. I snap my mirror shut.

'Daddy?'

'I know, baby. I know.'

I glance at the gas dial but it's more empty than full and anyway, we've got nothing to run from. Buck is straight as Abel now and when he walked out of prison yesterday it was through the front door. At the nearest gas station, we pull over and, before we can step out, the Oldsmobile swerves in front of us. There's a smell of exhaust and two plainclothes jump out with drawn shotguns. The attendant boy blinks fast, drops his pail of soapy water, and dips behind the pumps.

'Put your hands *up!*' the bigger of the men barks.

We do as we're told and they creep over to Buck's side of the sedan, opening the door slowly like they're half expecting him to blow their brains out. Then they tell Buck to get out and they start frisking him, messing up his good suit. After that come the accusations.

'Are you Clyde Barrow and Bonnie Parker?'

'No, sir!' Buck and me say at the same time.

'Well, you sure look the part.' The smaller one narrows his eyes at Buck. 'Got any proof?'

Buck says his papers are in the trunk and the officers exchange glances. Then the small one goes around while the big one stays with us, looking past Buck's shoulder at little old me inside the car. '*Bonnie Parker*. With my own eyes.'

I think, *he's going to be disappointed when he sees our papers*, but I don't say it. A few minutes later, the small one comes back around and he's shaking his head, laughing to himself like he can't believe our lucky stars, or their unlucky ones. 'He's a Barrow, but he ain't the one we want.'

'Clyde's my little brother,' Buck puffs himself up. If there's one thing I know about Barrows, it's that they're proud of being Barrows.

We make good time to Dallas, though we sure are rumpled from the road. In the little hotel room, we lie down in our day clothes and get even more rumpled. Then I guess I fall asleep, because the white walls are suddenly blue and I can see Buck's hat and shoes are gone. Though I know he wouldn't go far without me, it still hurts that he'd leave at all without so much as a note. I sit and sulk for a while then get up and do my makeup then go back to sulking when he still isn't back. He finally tiptoes in some twenty minutes later, slipping his shoes off at the door.

'Daddy, where'd you go?' I call through the darkness. Buck almost jumps out of his skin.

'Jeepers, baby!' He laughs. 'You were sleeping like a baby when I left.'

He takes off his hat and holds it to his heart, weaving slightly on his feet. Something drops inside me like a seat on a Ferris wheel. *Oh no*, I think. *Oh no, he hasn't.*

'Daddy, where were you?'

'I had to take a phone call, didn't I?'

'Have you been drinking?'

Buck looks offended, then starts grinning. 'Heck, nothing gets past you, baby. Go put on your shoes. I've got something to run by you, and I ain't doing it on an empty stomach.'

We go to the greasy spoon around the corner and both get the blue-plate special — cornbread and beef hash with two kinds of beans. Buck tries to sweeten me up by getting me to eat first, but as soon as Clyde's name comes up, I know it's bad. Dabbing gravy from his lips, Buck starts, 'You know, Clyde had this swell idea to bust Ray out of Eastham ...'

'*No*, Daddy.'

'That's what I told him. I said count me out, I ain't doing nothing that's gonna put Blanche and me at risk. He was beating his gums so long about it, saying how we know the country better'n them, and I said no. I said no, baby.'

'You did?'

'Sure. I ain't a complete sap. Thing is, him and Bonnie have had it hard lately, harder'n all of us. So I said we'd help them find a place to rest up …'

Buck starts painting a picture of how nice it'll be, the four of us living quietly somewhere for a few weeks. He says it'll be like a vacation, a family reunion almost, and Bonnie and I can fix the place up however we want. My eyes fill up. I pull my hand away from Buck's and shake my head, gathering up my white kid purse to go.

'It's supposed to be *us*, Daddy. We're supposed to be getting our own place.'

'Baby, we can do that anytime. I'm a free man, remember? Heck, don't go so fast! Don't you want some pudding?'

He really looks like he believes he's a free man too, fixing me with those shiny dark eyes. But I know there's no freedom where Clyde is concerned. The night is big and dirty and my legs too short to carry me far, but it's the least I can do to make him chase after me. He's dashing through the doors, setting his hat on crooked, grabbing for my arm.

'You know you mean more to me than anyone on heaven and earth, baby, family included! Why you gotta use that against me? Why you gotta be the only one in my life? Don't you know what a brother means to a brother?'

'If you meant as much to him, he wouldn't be asking.'

'You don't know that, baby. Lord, you don't know anything!'

'So now I'm *stupid*?' I turn around and cross my arms.

At that moment, another man starts walking up to the greasy spoon. He looks real down-and-out, with holes in his hat and his shirt stained the colour of hot chocolate. Buck hollers at the man.

'Stupid! Now she says I'm calling her stupid! No wonder a man drinks, friend! Say, friend, what say we find us the nearest speakeasy …'

'Hush, Daddy! Do you want to go back to the joint already?'

'What I want, baby, is to get us a nice little bungalow with trees all round and a car shop attached. But a man's got things he needs to do.'

They're staying at a tourist camp in Checotah, Oklahoma: Clyde and Bonnie and their buddy W.D., who's just a pug-nosed kid of sixteen. I wasn't expecting the kid, but I wasn't expecting to arrive so late either, with the sky so orange and dusty over the prairie grass. Clyde limps out to meet us in his shirtsleeves with a pick between his teeth, all smiles and shoulder-claps. 'Blanche-baby,' he bends down to kiss me. I don't want to like him, but as usual, I can't help it, especially with him looking so much like Buck and using Buck's pet name on me.

'How long you been here?' Buck asks Clyde as we're walking up to their cabin.

'Three nights.'

'And there ain't any heat?'

'There's always heat, brother, but it ain't too bad here. So long as we don't go to the grocery store. They got my poster up there.'

It's a nice brown-brick cabin with pale shutters pulled all the way down. When Clyde opens it up, I see Bonnie and W.D. huddled on the floor over a game of cards. They're both hardly dressed and the room is so dark and messy it looks like a tornado hit it, clothes and guns and cards scattered everywhere. Bonnie looks up and smiles so big I think her face is going to crack in half. She gets up to greet us, dragging her leg just like Clyde.

'I'm so glad! Bucky, you're *free*. And Blanche — it sure is good to see another gal.' Even though I'm not much over five foot myself, Bonnie has to lift her face way up to kiss me. I can smell the hooch on her breath. I look at her gimp leg and she says, 'Oh, Clyde crashed some car last year. I was pinned under. At least we both have limps now. If you ask me, he feels more man having me lame as well.'

'Doll, you'll always find a way to bring me down,' Clyde smiles. He puts his arm around Buck's shoulder. 'Come on, let me pour you something nasty.'

I don't much like whiskey, but I take a little and hold on to it while the others knock theirs right back. W.D. starts shuffling the cards, fancy like a magician. Bonnie reaches across the circle and refills everyone's glasses but mine. '*I'm* always happier when *I've* got something to drink,' she drawls, giving me this dippy sidelong smile. Up close, I can see the glossy black wing of her eyeliner, the silky flush of her cheeks. Even after a year of working at the Cinderella, I can't help goggling at how pretty she is.

'Buck, did Clyde tell you about our run-in with the law in Tarrant County? Oh, *boy*,' W.D.'s voice cracks on 'boy' and he takes a slurp of whiskey. 'It's a good 'un, I tell you.'

'Dry up, you sap. We don't wanna hear it.' Buck glances at me. I can tell from his face that he wouldn't mind hearing and is only humouring me. Honest to God, he treats me like I'm two years old sometimes.

Talk turns to Buck and Clyde's people after that, then to Bonnie's kid sister who W.D. is sweet on, then to the guys they know in Eastham. All the while, W.D. is dealing hands for poker and I'm trying to keep up, but I don't know how to play nor do I care for getting drunk. At last, I stand up and say I'm going to fix us all something to eat. Buck tries to stop me by getting hold of my ankles, but I kick him away.

As soon as I'm inside the kitchen, running myself a glass of water, I hear Buck asking in a low voice for that story. W.D. starts telling it in a whisper, too quiet for me to hear except for sound effects — *Biff! Fwoom! Kablammo!* — and their laughing.

All of them laughing, long into the night.

One thing I thank my lucky stars for is that Buck never gets violent when he's drinking. Not like my first husband, who used to bounce me against the walls and other things so awful I can't have children because of it. But Buck just gets stupid. Stupid, and darn pig-headed. Which I guess is its own special kind of dangerous.

We decide to set out as early as we can, though none of us have slept more than a wink. If you ask me, they're all still jazzed from last night. W.D. goes to settle the bill while I keep Bonnie company on the porch and our men pack the cars. When they're done, Clyde lifts Bonnie right up and carries her to the open roadster. Buck gets it in his head to carry me the same, though I don't have a limp and feel safer on my own than in the arms of a drunken man.

'Put me down, Daddy! Put me down!'

'Say "giddy-up", baby! C'mon, "giddy-up"!'

In the end, he sets me down, red in the face, a few feet from the car and slaps me on the rump. Then he walks over to the roadster and asks Clyde which way we're headed. Clyde looks at the sky. Instead of naming a point on the compass like we expect, he tells us, 'Joplin, Missouri.' Buck and me exchange looks.

'Why Joplin?'

'Good a place as any.' Clyde grins. Something about that grin makes me want to slap it right off his face. Instead, I straighten my dress and sigh myself into the sedan.

I try to get Buck to tell what might be in Joplin during the drive over, but all I get are grunts till finally he says he's got enough of a headache without me on his back. I know what he means by *headache*, bumping along the dirt road with that big Oklahoma sun shining down on us. Buck turns on the radio, but not even Rudy Vallée can make up for the stink we're both in.

Around two o'clock, we leave the others in some woods near a rest stop and go apartment hunting. Both of us cheer right up when we find a hideout a little ways outside town, in a near-empty stone block above a garage. Buck squeezes my hand and says, 'If this is how we feel now, imagine when we get a place of our own!' Which is just like Buck, making the best of a lousy situation.

Bonnie and me have some fun looking at linen samples I bring over from the five-and-dime in Joplin. I like gold but she likes green, and eventually talks me over to it, saying how it's more natural and harmonious. After I purchase some green drapes and pillows and so forth, she makes a big fuss saying how much she loves them, but loses interest when it comes to putting them in place. The same goes for the silverware and dishes, which Bonnie says she likes modern rather than fussy and delicate, yet barely gives a second glance to once they're inside the drawers.

I wasn't expecting Buck to pitch in much, but it's something else for a slip of a girl no different from myself to prefer polishing guns to silver. And she's got less taste in food than Buck. Maybe it's the smoking or maybe it's the whiskey, but both of them seem just as happy eating pickled trotters as a square meal.

'I don't know how they can stand them briny hogs' feet,' Clyde commiserates with me one night while I'm slicing potatoes in the kitchenette. He's leaning against the doorjamb in his shirtsleeves and vest, looking spiffy for someone who hasn't left the house in days. 'Can I lend a hand with the cooking there, Blanche?'

'Oh, *no*,' I tell him. 'You go right on back to your card game.'

But Clyde just grins like he knows better and eases up to the counter. 'If I keep staring at them cards, I'm gonna go cross-eyed. Honest.' He rolls up his sleeves and takes the knife from my hand. 'What're we making here? French fried?'

'French fried and chipped beef with cream and onions.'

As it turns out, Clyde is pretty handy with a knife and cutting board. And he likes things nice and neat, same as me. A little while into cooking, W.D. comes in to see what's going on. He doesn't like being apart from either Clyde or Bonnie long, if he can help it, and even sleeps on the floor of their room rather than alone on the sofa.

'Oh, boy, you make it with onions?' he asks. 'My ma never done *that*.'

From that night on, Clyde usually gives me a hand in the

kitchen. It's not the same as having another woman to help, but it does make me a little sweeter on him, and less bent up about their bad habits. For folks trying to keep a low profile, they sure do make a lot of noise playing poker and drinking till all hours.

Though I do more than anyone around the apartment, I've never felt lazier in my life. Not a day goes by that we don't stay in bed past midday. Buck is to blame, always waking up so warm and smoochy. I feel bad because the walls are so thin, but certain things just happen between married people. One day we end up rising later than the rest and they're all lounging around already on the hooch. I ask how they slept and they say 'Swell!', but when my back is turned, Bonnie whispers, '… *if it weren't for all your darn baby-making.*'

Well, Buck knows that's a sore point for me. Right away, he spirits me out of the room and tries to calm me, but he has a hard time getting me to stop crying.

'Shh, baby. Bonnie don't know no better. She don't know you or me,' he says. 'She's probably jealous her and Clyde aren't so close as us. They always got W.D. with them.'

'At least they c-can h-have a baby!' I sob.

'In this life? Like heck. They wouldn't know what to do with it.' Buck hugs me. 'Besides, baby, you're the only one *I* need. I don't want some goo-goo ga-ga kid getting all your attention.'

Buck keeps saying sweet things till the tears stop. Then he just holds me for a while. After that, he kisses my hot forehead and tells me to get myself cleaned up. 'Thank you, Daddy,' I say when he's at the door.

I can hear voices coming from the other room and know they're talking about me. A little while later, Bonnie raps on the door and asks if she can come in. By then, I'm sitting at the vanity powdering my face. She sits down beside me. She doesn't say anything about babies nor does she apologise, but I can tell she's trying to make it up.

'Blanche, you've got the loveliest skin. I'm so darn freckle-faced *and* I don't know what to do with myself,' she marvels, though I can't see a single spot on her face. 'I don't know how you do it!'

'Oh,' I say coolly. 'It's just a matter of having a good regime.'

'Regime? What kind of regime?'

Despite myself, I tell her: Pond's cold cream, a tonic of witch-hazel and rosewater, and regular home remedies for blemishes. There's a complexion mask made of lemon and baking soda that I like to use weekly. Bonnie smiles and nods in all the right places and keeps asking questions, and even jokes that we should test it on W.D., who's got the worst skin of anyone. When she suggests I do her makeup, I agree quicker than I mean to. I'd never tell Buck, but some days I miss the Cinderella.

'Gee, it's a pity to look this good with nowhere to go,' Bonnie says later, when we're both blinking in the mirror like a pair of kewpie dolls, one light and one dark. 'Maybe we should hit the town.'

'We can't do *that* —' I begin. She cuts in.

'Why not? Heck, the guys won't miss us, and I'm sick to death of being all cooped up. It makes me cuckoo! Come on …' I shake my head but she keeps talking me over. 'Nobody's gonna recognise me, if that's what worries you. Clyde's the one with his mug plastered everywhere. Me? I'm *in-cog-ni-to*.' Again, she primps in the mirror. 'They're more likely to mistake me for Jean Harlow than Bonnie Parker.'

We have a real gals' day: the new Clark Gable matinee and, after that, pie and shopping at the five-and-dime. We buy matching finger-rings and ear-screws, only twenty cents together. 'Do you ever feel like you're living in a movie?' Bonnie asks me, twirling her ring. I don't know what she means, and I wonder if she's still jazzed from earlier, but I just tell her, 'Maybe when I'm real dolled up.'

It's almost dark by the time we come up the stairs. I can't hear the usual noise of poker and radio music. When Bonnie unlocks the door there's no sign of the guys, and the only smoke I can smell is stale, like they stubbed out their cigars hours ago.

'Don't get in a stink.' Bonnie's eyes squint out from her makeup: two mean, pale slivers. 'They probably had some business to do.'

The guys get back early that morning with a bag of stolen guns — and drunk, to boot. Bonnie actually squeals when she sees the machine gun and jumps right into Clyde's arms, smooching him all over like she wants to start some baby-making of her own. Buck looks guilty when he gets to the bottom of the bag and says, 'Don't think I've forgotten you, baby.' Then he pulls out a pair of field glasses.

'You're our lookout, Blanche-baby!' Clyde calls out between Bonnie's kisses.

It's near five o'clock on our last night in Joplin and I'm fixing to do a big load of washing. The guys are down in the garage ready-ing the cars. The last I saw of Bonnie, she was in her kimono, smoking a Camel cigarette and writing poetry. She's been in a quiet mood since Buck and me said we're leaving; I don't know if she's glad or sour about it and, honest to God, I don't care.

I dump the clothes in the water with some soap powder. Through the floor, I can hear the guys slamming shut the trunk. Then there's a different kind of slam outside the garage. Before I can go to the window to look, the ground starts rumbling beneath me and Bonnie flies past the kitchen with her gun drawn. 'Get a move on, you!' she screeches. 'Get everything, now!'

It's hard to know which way to run or what she means by 'everything'. I'm scrambling around for our purses while Bonnie fires shots from behind the curtains. Then W.D. rushes up from the garage holding his side and crying, 'I'm dyin'! I'm dyin'!' I take him by the waist and crouch with him in a corner, his blood seeping into my sprigged cotton dress. When the shooting stops, Buck charges upstairs. His shirt is splattered red, but he doesn't seem to be hurting.

'We have to go, baby! This instant!'

'Is Clyde shot?' Bonnie grabs his sleeve. Buck shakes her off.

'Baby, now! Bonnie, help us with W.D., will you?'

We all stumble downstairs together, W.D. still crying about the wound in his side. The garage is full of bullet holes and on the floor is a man in a blue suit with a red mess where his head should be. At first, I think it's Clyde and I guess so does Bonnie because she gives an awful sob. But then we see Clyde crouching behind the sedan with his rifle pointed at the street. He's got a look on his face that I'll never forget — like he's a few pieces away from finishing a jigsaw puzzle.

'Gals, go in the back with W.D.,' he whispers. 'Buck, help me move this thing.'

We do as he says, helping W.D. into the back as Buck pushes and Clyde keeps his rifle pointed. When the sedan starts rolling downhill, they dash to the front, outrunning a new hail of bullets. I'm holding my head and screaming, 'Daddy!' and W.D. is crying, 'I'm dyin'! I'm really dyin'!' Buck's got the wheel and is hurtling down the street as Clyde aims and shoots, aims and shoots.

I never thought things were perfect in Joplin, but being on the road makes me realise how good we had it. At least in Joplin we were living like human beings. But this life is no better than an animal's, just running and hiding and hungering and dirt.

We even fight like animals. There's hardly an hour when one of us isn't at another's throat, and the rest of us trying to keep them apart. Clyde and Buck are always arguing about the way to do things I'd rather we didn't have to do, and I argue with Buck about going home, and Bonnie argues with everyone about darn near everything. Honest to God, I've never met such a hellcat. She even picks on W.D., once he's healed.

'Stop your drooling!' She shoves him off her shoulder where he's fallen asleep, one afternoon. 'Can't you even *sleep* without being a darn slob? You're dumber'n a dog, you are!'

We drive up to Illinois, Indiana, Iowa, Nebraska, back down through Kansas and home-state Texas. I use some cash from one of their stickups to buy hats for the men, breeches for me and Bonnie, boots for us all. Wherever we can, we pick up newspapers. The laws found some film in the camera Bonnie left back in Joplin and now they have a mug to print next to her name, along with some pictures of the two of them clowning with their guns. I'm still 'unidentified female', but they've got Buck's name and seeing it is like losing him to the joint all over again.

'You should go home while you can, baby,' he tells me at a camp outside Waco. 'I'll put you on a bus right now. You'll be back with your folks by nightfall.'

I think of my poor old pa, deaf in one ear, and the little Okie church where he preaches to other farmers. But there's no leaving Buck, no matter how much he tries to baby me, no matter how much bickering, dirt, and tears. This is the life we've been given, and if anything makes us better than animals, it's each other.

Things start looking up when Buck steals a Ford coupe for the two of us. It sure is good not to be crammed in with the others all the time, and the car is small enough that I can drive it, letting Buck get some shut-eye for a change.

With Buck snoring beside me, and their car just a speck on the horizon, I sometimes think how easy it would be to lose them. Slow right down and find another road, because no road can be worse than the one we're on. But my hands stay glued to the wheel, and we keep eating their dust. I guess I don't like the thought of betraying anyone's trust, whether they're deserving or not.

Clyde trusts us so much that he even gets us to wait across the state line while they do a job in Wellington. It's an hour's drive of mostly red dirt, and we make it to the bridge where we're fixing to meet with no cash and a long time to spare. Buck parks a little way off and we take a walk by the dry creek bed, pitching stones across it.

'Want to lie in those bushes a while, baby?' he asks me. I look at the low, prickly bushes he means and say, 'Nuh-uh, Daddy.' Further up the path, we see a copperhead sunning itself and turn back.

By dark, there's still no sign of the others. We park closer to the bridge and take turns with the field glasses, but there's nothing to see. After some time, we wrap ourselves in a picnic blanket and fall asleep. Then it's late and there's a horn honking and a pair of headlights flashing on the bridge. 'Jeepers,' Buck coughs. He starts rolling the car forward. I wipe the sleep from my eyes and pick up the field glasses.

'Clyde,' I say softly.

Through the dark, I can see him running with his shotgun, away from what looks like a law car. He reaches us and starts banging on our window, his eyes big and crazy. There's blood coming from his nose, and his face is all cut up.

'Bonnie's dyin'! We gotta move her! I killed two laws! There's two more tied up we gotta get rid of!'

Buck rushes out. I start to do the same and Clyde stops me. 'Not you. They ain't seen you yet.' He leans his bloody face against the door. 'See if you can't find something to make Bonnie comfortable. Oh, God, she's gonna *die* …'

He's back at their car as quickly as he came, and Buck and W.D. are bearing Bonnie across the bridge. I get out to help them lay her down and it's bad — she doesn't look like Bonnie so much as a mess of cuts and burns. Her leg is the worst, black and bubbly like a toasted marshmallow.

'Keep fightin', sis,' Buck whispers to her. Then he gallops back over the bridge to help Clyde with the laws.

I remember Pa telling me how they used to put blankets on the soldiers who'd been blasted in the trenches, to keep them from catching fever. So I spread that picnic blanket over Bonnie. As I'm doing it, my fingers brush against her half-melted high heel, and I know it's mean, but I can't help flinching.

In a small-town drugstore, I buy us some tape, bandages, and medicine. Clyde won't go to a hospital or even send for a doctor till the heat is down, though he stands to lose the most if Bonnie dies. She's in and out of sleep, and moaning, and even gets the shakes overnight. We keep driving through to Arkansas. In Fort Smith, Clyde finds a backstreet doctor who cleans out the black skin and gives her a tetanus shot and some Amytal for the pain.

I guess the dope gives Bonnie something to live for. She starts talking after that, first just asking for her ma, then telling Clyde how much she loves him. Her voice doesn't sound any more like her than her face looks it, but thankfully there's more that he loves about her than her face and voice. 'Doll, you're love itself,' he says, stroking her hand — one of the few parts of her not burnt or cut up.

We stay more than a week in Fort Smith. I cook and shop and

do laundry while Buck and W.D. do small-time jobs. By the end of it, Bonnie's leg is looking brown and sinewy, like the mummy I once saw at a travelling freak show, and she's got her fight back. More than ever, maybe.

I'm getting breakfast ready one morning when I hear her cussing the guys through the walls. 'Send that hellcat in!' she's screaming. 'I'm gonna whip her! I hate her guts!'

Well, I don't know what I did to earn the name 'hellcat', but I go in, breakfast tray and all. Bonnie's teeth show through the redness of her face. 'You!' she yells, leaping forward. 'I *hate* you! I'm gonna whip you, this minute!'

I look at our men, but they don't seem to have any more idea than I do. 'I ain't fightin' you,' I tell her, putting down the tray.

'That's because you're fraidy! Damn fraidy-cat!' she jeers. 'You can't do nothing useful! You or Buck! You two are burdens, is what you are! Good for nothing, just complainin', complainin'!' Bonnie spits at her breakfast. 'You're like listening to a broken record! *Baby-daddy, baby-daddy, baby-daddy.* Clyde and me, we'd be better without you!'

'Like heck,' I say. Near dead or not, there's such a thing as gratitude.

'*Baby-daddy, baby-daddy! Oh, it's so hard being widdle baby me …*'

I turn to Buck and raise my hands. 'Daddy, she's crackers.'

'*Daddy, she's crackers.* What'd I tell you? You, you … baby! I'll whip you! Clyde'll whip Buck! Look! He'll do it! He *loves* me!'

'Buck loves *me*,' I say. 'He won't let himself get whipped.'

'You miserable sap! He'll do it!'

'Is this what you gals fight about?' Buck shakes his head. 'Lordy …'

'You better close your head too, Buck! If it wasn't for Clyde, you'd be nothing! You'd still be stealing turkeys!'

She keeps screaming for some five minutes till I finally burst into tears. 'I hope you choke!' I tell her. Then I storm out of the room. Buck follows.

'Baby, don't fuss, you know she ain't right —'

'Oh!' I sob. 'She's *never* been right!'

One night Buck and W.D. do a job in Fayetteville. It isn't a big one, but they don't get back till late and both are real shook up and bloody. 'Daddy!' I scream when I see them. Buck lets me throw my arms around him, but it takes some coaxing before he tells me, 'Baby, I believe I killed a man.'

We drive nonstop to Missouri with Buck and Clyde bickering all the way. Buck's had it with Clyde's bullying; he says he's a rat, and we'll go our own way as soon as it's safe. Clyde smirks till Buck is out of breath. Then he calls him fraidy, and I swear they darn near kill us all, the way Buck goes for Clyde's throat and the car swerving and Bonnie with her cut-up face screaming, 'Let me out! I hate you all! I wish we were dead already!'

At the motor court, we rent separate cabins with a garage between them. I don't like the way people stare at my breeches and riding boots, but once we're alone, Buck sits me on the bed and pulls the boots from my feet. Later, freshly showered and shining them in his undershirt, he asks me, 'How'd you like to go to Canada?'

23

'I'll go anywhere that isn't here,' I say.

'We'll get us a log cabin and be fur trappers.' Buck smiles. 'Bears, beavers, coons …'

'Sure, Daddy.' But there's something that's been bothering me since Bonnie screamed at us in the car. 'Daddy … if I got killed, what would you do?'

He stops shining. 'Why, baby, I couldn't go on living.'

That's what I expected, but it doesn't please me to hear. 'I don't want you to do that. I want you to leave me someplace where I'll be found and given a proper burial, and then I want you to keep going —'

'Baby, don't let's talk about this.' Buck drops the cloth and comes to my side. 'You know I couldn't just leave you any old place.'

Then he asks me what I'd do if it was him.

'I'd stay with you as long as I'm alive,' I say. 'Till the laws come and separate us.'

We sit quietly a while, Buck's arms around my shoulders. I wish we weren't so skinny. When we hear someone banging out-side our cabin, we both jump, and I know he's thinking the same thing I am: that the laws have come to separate us already.

Actually, it's just Clyde, asking if I can go across the court and buy them some fried chicken and beer.

We're woken in the night by a light flashing on our windows, a pounding on the door. '*Daddy*,' I whisper. Buck's eyelashes flut-ter. The door keeps pounding. I jump over the foot of the bed and start dragging on my breeches. '*Daddy … what should I say?*'

Buck sits up, long-faced in the dark. 'Ask who it is and what they want.' He yawns, but I know from his voice he's more scared than all that. 'Stall 'em as best you can.'

He starts putting on his trousers as I tiptoe to the door. I open it a crack and they shine a light in my face, so bright I can't see.

'Who *are* you?' I ask.

'We're the law,' says the man in front. As my sight flashes off and on, I notice his brown uniform.

'Well … What do you want?'

'We want you to send out your men.'

'There ain't no men *here*.'

'Step outside yourself then, ma'am.'

I glance at Buck, tucking his trousers into his boots. He murmurs something and I repeat it, loud and clear. 'The. Men. Are. In. The. Other. Cabin.'

'Step outside, ma'am.'

'I ain't dressed,' I snap. 'Can I put some clothes on, at least?'

The laws look at each other. I wonder if there are more hidden nearby. 'Be quick about it.'

I turn around and bump right into Buck. He's slipping his pistol into his belt, reaching for the rifle leaning by the sofa. 'Stay close as you can to the wall,' he says. 'I sure am sorry, but I'm gonna have to kill those men.'

Before Buck can do anything, there's a revving and a ramming outside the garage. A bullet flies through the window nearest Buck and he shoves me against the wall. I cross my arms over my face as bits of plaster and mirror explode. Then the shooting stops as soon as it started and the car that was ramming the garage backs out, sounding its horn like a hurt goose.

'Aw, hell. They're calling more laws.' Buck lowers his rifle and cocks his head to the cabin wall. 'Hey, brother, you alright?'

'Yeah,' Clyde calls. 'Let's get outta here.'

I try to grab for the door handle, but Buck shoves me aside again, mutters, 'Don't, baby! You'll get killed! Go after I go!'

It seems to me we'll both be dead before we stop arguing about who gets to face the fire first.

We hear Clyde's motor start. Buck gives the word and pushes out before me. Clyde and W.D. are already at the wheel of the Ford, cocking their rifles as Bonnie hops in on her one good leg. I keep my eyes on Buck's back, broad like a shield. Out of nowhere, a shot pings past my head.

Buck falls.

Buck falls, and he's bleeding.

'Daddy!' I go down to my knees.

'I dropped my gun ...' Buck mumbles, right before he passes out.

All of us are squashed into the car and Clyde is backing out of camp as fast as he can. I'm trying to keep Buck's eyes open, his head from rolling. 'Daddy, it's me. Daddy, wake up ...' It's hard sapping the tears from my voice when I can feel his head leaking. Clyde tells me to keep talking like I am. I don't know how he can be so calm, but it makes me feel better about getting Buck out safe — that is, till the bullets start raining again.

'Hell!' Clyde cusses, not so calm anymore.

Glass smashes, and something hard streaks across my forehead. I can't see anything, but I'm covering Buck's face, screaming as more sharp things fly at us. The car swerves. I try to see if Buck has been shot again but everything stays dark and there's hotness dripping from my eyes, too thick to be tears.

'I'm blind,' I say. Nobody seems to hear me.

I don't know which way we turn or how far we drive, only that it gets quiet after a while. Clyde says something about a flat tire and there's cussing then more quiet as the car slows. I pipe up asking if they can check on Buck. 'Why can't you do it?' Bonnie asks.

'I'm *blind*,' I say again.

They get out of the car and someone starts on the tyre — W.D., I think. Someone else strikes a match and holds it to my face. 'There's a lotta blood,' Clyde says. 'But the eyeballs ain't busted.' I hear Bonnie striking a match near Buck and ask how bad he is. She doesn't answer at first. I ask again.

'Well, it ain't deep enough to kill him …' She pauses. 'But it's in there.'

My eyes start flooding and Clyde says, 'That's good. See if you can't cry some of that glass out.' He starts dabbing at the blood and water. I see a fuzz of light where the match is and try to focus on it, not the silence around Buck. Then he starts groaning.

'Baby. My head hurts …'

'Daddy!' I feel my way to him. 'Keep talking.'

'My head hurts, baby …' he says again. 'Can you take my hat off?'

'Not yet.' I stroke the bloody fabric tied around his head. 'You gotta keep it on till we get home.'

If he wasn't willing to stop at a hospital for Bonnie, Clyde sure as hell won't for Buck, but that doesn't keep me from begging as we drive all night and all the next day. Clyde keeps shaking his head. Finally, he turns around.

'You think they're going to treat *my* brother? Blanche-baby, they'd sooner put another bullet in him.'

The truth hits me then. How many laws has Buck killed? Three, four? Not so many as Clyde, but enough to get a bounty on his head. My big, soft-hearted Buck, who's never raised a hand to me, even on the hooch.

That afternoon, we stop in a wooded area somewhere in Iowa. I can tell it's woods because the light in my eyes is greenish instead of brown and there's a twittering of little birds. Clyde takes out one of the car cushions and spreads it under a tree for Buck. I sit by him as the sky turns and the air gets colder, wetting his lips and checking his pulse whenever he gets too quiet.

'Lie down, baby,' he tells me, every time he comes to. 'Lie down on the grass with me. You know I'm hurtin'.'

But I'm too scared to lie down, in case I close my eyes and wake up with a dead man.

Clyde makes a fire that night. By the light of it, he picks more glass from my eyes, but there's a big piece in one of my pupils that just won't budge. Neither him nor Bonnie can get a grip on it and it hurts so bad that I'd rather they left it alone. So they give me some drops and bandage it up again. No one touches the wound in Buck's head, except to pour in hydrogen peroxide and change the dressing.

Later, I hear some noise past the fire, like dirt being moved. When I call out asking what it is, the men don't answer; only Bonnie comes and sits down beside me. 'This place ain't so bad, sis,' she says. 'It's kinda pretty. Peaceful-like.' Then she offers to watch Buck for the night.

I stay up with him, though, as the others curl up next to the embers. There are whippoorwills hunting in the trees and a screech owl that won't quit screeching, even when W.D. throws an empty bean can at it. 'How the heck do animals sleep out here?' Bonnie gripes, forgetting all her talk of peacefulness. But soon enough, W.D. is snoring. I can't say for sure, but I think Bonnie and Clyde start canoodling after that.

I guess I fall asleep because the next thing I know, I'm woken up by Buck jabbering. 'Gimme my pistol, baby,' he's saying, pawing at my lap. 'I gotta shoot them soldiers.'

I don't see any soldiers, but then I remember it's night-time and I'm blind on top of that. My heart starts beating real fast and I get an awful taste in my mouth, part nerves and part sickness over how bad Buck's head is smelling.

'There's soldiers?' I ask. 'Where?'

'Shh. In the woods. They's gonna kill us.' He goes quiet for a minute. 'They's all around us, baby!'

All the light from the fire is gone, and I can smell the cold ashes. I listen out for some sign of the others, but the only sound is my breathing and Buck's, shallow and wet. I wonder whether if I shut my eyes tight enough, it might be possible to dream the two of us back to that night of the open window and the blowing hackberry tree. Then I hear it, unmistakable: a gun clicking somewhere nearby.

'Gimme my pistol, baby,' Buck says, softer this time.

Eva

According to my sister Ilse, there's a Jew in Vienna who spends all his time listening to bored women talking. They lie down on a couch with their backs to him, plucking at their blouse buttons and going on about all sorts of things: their dreams, their memories, their childhoods.

'Why?' I ask Ilse.

'For enlightenment,' she says. 'Of course, *you* wouldn't know anything about that.'

Ilse is working for a Jewish doctor when she tells me this. His name is Dr Marx and he's an ear, nose, and throat specialist. He lets her sleep in a room next to his office and she stops going out with young men, spouts off about apnea and sinusitus whenever she gets the chance. When things start changing and Dr Marx has to move to America, Ilse's eyes are red for weeks. She looks at me like she hates me and says it's all my fault, that things could be different if I weren't so ignorant.

Sometimes I think about that Jew in Vienna when I'm lying

around, waiting for Him. By the phone in my little brown-roofed villa. On the terrace beneath the bright umbrellas. Smoking in my suite at the Grand Hotel. I think about my head opening up and everything spilling out of it in a multicoloured jumble, like clothes on the floor when I'm dressing for dinner. My dreams. My memories. My childhood. All of it falling together until I'm enlightened.

It begins on a couch. In the drawing room of his Prince Regent's Place apartment, with Him in mourning and me giddy from a half-bottle of champagne. He won't drink, but I'm determined to cheer him up. I lean on his arm on our way out of the restaurant and, in the Mercedes, blink at him with serious eyes. I tell him I'd do anything to see him happy.

It is quick and less painful than I expect. Embarrassing in its quickness, like a fish leaping into a rowboat, thrashing about, then sliding back into the deep blue water. His face turns red, like I've heard it does when he makes speeches. Once he has caught his breath and buttoned up, he rises from the couch. I pull down my dress and start rolling on my stockings, but they're full of runs. He touches my golden head and tells me he'll buy me new ones. He tells me I'm a good girl.

Before the beginning, I'm working as an assistant at Mr Hoffman's photo studio. I've only been there three weeks, but it's the longest job I've had out of convent school, and the work isn't bad — at least, not as boring as typing. He comes in while I'm on a ladder, reaching for some files on the top shelf and wearing a skirt that's hemmed too short. He stands at the front of the shop, wearing a shabby raincoat and talking to Mr Hoffmann in a low voice. I can feel them looking at my legs.

I don't recognise Him from his photographs. I don't recognise any of the men who come in, though I see their faces every day in the darkroom. But after I come down from the ladder that day and he asks for my name and kisses my hand, I start paying attention. I can't say why, but I feel like I have to.

Every time He comes into the shop, he makes a point of talking to me. It surprises me that he takes such an interest, him being so much older and serious-looking, me the youngest girl at work and still plump from my convent-school diet. But when we start talking, I find out he's not so serious. He likes to eat cream cakes and marzipan. He likes to go to the theatre. He likes to pay compliments to pretty girls, me most of all.

How lovely your complexion is, Miss Eva! Like peaches and cream.

Those stockings look very nice, Miss Eva. You have the legs of a dancer.

Miss Eva, you should be in front of a camera, not behind one!

One day, He brings me an autographed photo of himself in uniform, looking mysterious and thoughtful. I show the photograph to Ilse when I get home from work and she laughs so much I want to slap her, then tells me solemnly that I can't let Papa see it. 'You know how he feels about radical politics,' she says. Together we lift up the lining of my underwear drawer and hide it beneath my schoolgirl wools and cottons. For now, I can only dream of satin and lace.

~

Sometimes, my papa says I'm a good girl. Other times, he says I'm bad, wayward, a disappointment. I can be good for getting a B in German. I can be bad for getting a B in German. I can be good for looking pretty. I can be bad for looking pretty. I can be good for playing sports like a boy. I can be bad for playing sports like a boy. It's so hard for me to keep track of what's good and what's bad, I've given up trying.

Ilse never gets in trouble with Papa. Neither does my little sister Gretl, who's still at the convent. It's only me who seems to get Papa worked up. One night at the dinner table, I ask Papa if he's heard of Him, just to see how he reacts.

'That man? He's a charlatan, a fool who thinks he's omniscient. He says he's going to change the world. Not likely!'

Ilse and I stuff our cheeks full of potato so Papa won't see us laughing, and are quick to go our own ways once our plates are cleared. I think she's sneaking out to call Dr Marx. I shut the door to our room and lie down, closing my eyes until I can see His face floating above mine. I see his face and it's like lying in a field of forget-me-nots, under a full white moon, at the height of spring. I say his name and feel bad, delicious.

He often has to go out of town for business, to the capital and other places. Sometimes, months pass without me seeing him. This is okay before what happens on the couch, but afterward, I assume things will be different. I wonder what the point of it all is — his compliments and gifts, his dates with me to the theatre and opera and his chalet in the mountains — if he has so little need of me. I stop being plump.

He had a niece who lived at his Prince Regent's Place apartment before he and I become lovers. She was pretty and round-faced, and wore the latest fashions from Vienna — clicky heels and fur coats, beautiful silk dresses. One day, when he was off working somewhere else, she aimed a pistol at her chest and shot herself dead.

I remember this when I am alone in my parents' house, waiting for a phone call that never comes. Unlocking Papa's war pistol from its dusty case and pointing it where I hurt most, then jerking it away right before it goes off. Ilse comes home first, finds me dizzy in a puddle of my own blood. She calls one of Dr Marx's friends and he fixes me up in the middle of the night. We pass the whole thing off to my parents as an accident.

And Him? He flies back immediately and promises me an apartment of my own, close to his.

Papa and He first meet when I'm on tour with his publicity team. I set up equipment for my boss and sometimes get to take photos of Him myself, making speeches and holding his hand up to the crowds. The crowds are always full of women, who give off a bad smell and yell out crazy things — that they love him, that they would die for him, that they want to bear his children. I'm not jealous of these women. They'll never get as close to him as me.

We stop at a lodge outside town. I tell my parents to be there for lunch, though our convoy doesn't arrive until after four. Papa is civil. He hails him, and afterward they shake hands. 'Your daughter is a very good girl,' He tells Papa. Papa says nothing. He knows exactly what this means.

I don't want to be ignorant, but politics are so boring to me. Every time I try to get through the book He wrote before he became famous, it's like being back at convent-school among the stink of Bible pages. It's the same with the newspapers, which I only skim for pictures of Him. And music. I'd rather dance to fast jazz or slow, moony American love songs than listen to the stuff He likes: Strauss, Verdi, Wagner, Wagner, Wagner.

He doesn't mind if I'm ignorant. I can sit in the sun and read Oscar Wilde, flick through fashion and movie magazines, and he's happy. He says it's better for a woman to be soft, sweet, and stupid than intellectual, and I don't want to argue. I don't want to be like Ilse, always trying to sound smarter than she really is.

He gives me the brown-roofed villa after I take too many sleeping pills on purpose. My papa won't visit me there, but Mama and Ilse do. We drink nice wine and I show them the flagstone patio, the table-tennis set, the high garden walls that no busybodies can see over. I show them all the artwork on the walls inside, including some watercolours that He did himself a long time ago. I show them the brand-new TV set, which gets broadcasts straight from the capital. I tell Ilse she's welcome to move in with me along with our little sister Gretl, who's coming home from convent in a few weeks. She isn't interested. Dr Marx is still in town, running his practice.

He gives me two little black dogs to keep me company in the villa, which follow me around as eagerly as Gretl does. He gives me a monthly allowance and I spend it on pretty things from Vienna and Italy: crocodile leather, silk underwear, shoes by Ferragamo. Nowadays, I don't work unless he is going somewhere and wants me along as an assistant. Instead, Gretl and I lie on my bed during the day looking at patterns and catalogues, and picking out what will suit me best.

Sometimes, I think of hurting myself again: not only when He is out of town for too long, but also when he's *in* town and cold-shouldering me in public, telling everyone that he'll never marry, that the only woman in his life is Germany. I think of doing it with poison, like Madame Bovary. But then I remember the fairytales I grew up with, and how everything happens in threes. Three is serious. It's life or death.

In summer, Gretl and I hitch rides in the mail truck out to the Königssee, where the waters are the same deep blue as His eyes and icy with reflected snowcaps. There are always bronze-backed young men by the lake whom we have fun with: men with corn-silk hair and names like Rudi, Heini, Bruno. They flick us with their towels, dunk us underwater and bear us up again in their strong arms.

He isn't jealous when he sees pictures of me in my swimsuit with the young men. He says it's good to see me having fun, making the most of the long summer days. He says there's nothing more virtuous in the world than young, healthy, German bodies having fun in the sunlight.

They are German men, His men. I don't forget this, even when they grab me by the wrists and ankles and swing me into the water, so I hit its surface with a hard, thrilling slap. My heart breaks as pleasure ripples through me — a murky bubbling and a pure mountain sky. They help me up and I know it's all just innocent fun, know that their bodies belong to Him as much as mine does.

In dreams, familiar things look unfamiliar. Places I know now seem too big, like I'm seeing them through the eyes of a child, while places I knew back then are too small to fit me. I wander through the empty studio, the rooms of the Grand Hotel, as if I'm the only person left on earth. I sit cramped at my school desk or on the floor of my parents' apartment, among a clutter of cheap furniture and flowered wallpaper. No matter where I am, I can't get comfortable.

There's one dream where I'm lying on the terrace of the Grand Hotel, looking at the view of the mountains. It's winter and no one else is out, but I can feel Him standing right behind my chair. I long to turn around and look at him, but I have a feeling that it's strictly forbidden, that I'll see something terrible if I do.

All sorts of people come to see Him at the Grand Hotel — not just politicians and military men, but royalty, film stars, musicians. Sometimes I'm allowed to dine with these guests in the big hall, posing as a secretary. Other times, I'm confined to my suite while his real secretaries get to stay at the table.

I don't understand what makes Him decide when to lock me

away. In my suite, I throw clothes off their racks; I smoke and pace. I flop down on my chintz couch and feel so bored it aches.

He has a separate suite, with a narrow iron bed and a neat little adjoining office. I don't go into his rooms, but he comes into mine — usually close to dawn, when his face is grey and his eyelids drooping and pouched. I don't look as he shuffles up to the bed in his billowy nightshirt, knowing he's embarrassed of his unshelled body, the soft belly and narrow shoulders beneath his padded uniform. As soon as he gets under the sheets, however, I turn my gold toward him. I am the sun, breaking over the mountains.

My whole family comes to visit me at the Grand Hotel, Papa included. We ride out of the gates on bicycles, wearing feathered hats with crisp shirts and slacks. My little black dogs chase after us, yapping as we roll down the grassy slopes. Everyone is happy and everyone is here as my guest, breathing luxury instead of the stale air of their tiny apartment back in town.

Papa has changed his mind about His politics. He now has a uniform of his own, which he wears to lunch in the great dining hall. He wears it back in town, too, for the family portrait we sit for on his sixtieth birthday. It is September and there is a lot going on in the east that's keeping Him busy, but everyone says it will be over soon.

When He is away from the Grand Hotel, I have to be on my guard. Other women, officials' wives, lie like snakes in the sun, coils glistening and chins held high. Other men, fat officials and lean younger officers, hedge me in hallways with their hot hands and breath. They don't expect to succeed, but they linger over my body like they hope to leave a mark, then stride back into the open and joke about what a stupid little flirt I am.

I don't tell Him about all this when he calls; if he calls. He has enough to worry about without me coming to him with my petty troubles. Instead, I keep Gretl with me, long after the rest of my family has gone back to town. I invite my old school friends to visit with their children, and pretty blonde Marion, who used to be an opera singer. We sit apart from the other women, tanning ourselves and taking pictures of one another looking chic and sun-kissed. In our bathing suits, we practice yoga and gymnastics, feats of flexibility that make the men stare and their wives shoot daggers.

When He is back, I make the Grand Hotel feel like a home. He appreciates my efforts: the cut flowers I bring in from the fields, the photo slides and home-video footage I show on the evenings he wants a break from work. 'There's me by the lake doing yoga. That's called a wheel pose,' I tell him. 'And here's us tanning our backs.' The wives yawn and sneer, but He claps his hands. *Beautiful*, he says. *It's beautiful to be home.*

I haven't tried to hurt myself again and haven't thought about it either. There's so much going on right now and I have so much to look forward to, once all His work is done. He says the end of his work is almost in sight, and Germany will soon triumph. The world will be a more beautiful place after we triumph, and He will finally be free to retire. He tells me we will have a big wedding then, and everyone will know I'm the only woman in his life.

I know He worries about me hurting myself, not just on purpose, but also by accident. He worries about me not eating enough. He worries about me when I'm skiing and skating, doing high dives and swinging upside-down from my exercise bar. He worries about me getting cancer from bathing in the sun too long, and from the cigarettes I won't give up. He worries about his enemies hurting me as a way of getting to him, keeping me hostage and interrogating me for information I don't have.

I worry about Him, too. He wasn't young when we met, but now he is over fifty, with shaking hands and a sensitive tummy and a hunched, shuffling walk. There are lots of bad people who want to see him dead, and it's taking a toll on him, even if he likes to joke about exploding podiums and bombed hotels. One summer, when he's working in his Eastern headquarters, a bomb goes off in the conference room just feet from where he's sitting. He escapes with a perforated eardrum and a shredded uniform, which he sends to me as a trophy.

Soon after Dr Marx moves away, Ilse marries a lawyer, divorces, then marries another lawyer. Gretl gets married, too, a couple of years later, to a dashing general called Hermann. She is crazy for his broad shoulders and luscious lips, which she tries out within weeks of him arriving at the Grand Hotel. Neither of them know anything about true love. All the same, they look good dancing together at the wedding, hand in hand and cheek to cheek.

I dance with Hermann, too, almost as close and almost as

much. If it weren't for me, Gretl would never have found a husband like him, or been able to afford a wedding like this. We feast high up in the mountains, in the eyrie above the Grand Hotel. An accordion man and two violinists serenade us with gypsy songs.

Though He foots the bill and makes an appearance at the ceremony, he doesn't stay for the celebrations and he certainly doesn't dance. There is still work to be done.

I think of us dancing on that mountaintop, like heroes in Valhalla, when we are hiding in the concrete world underground. Only a year has passed, but so much has crumbled, so much is closing in around us. While He sleeps, as still and grey as a corpse, I get everyone to come out of the shelter with me, to the empty rooms upstairs. There is champagne and a gramophone, a song about happiness and blood-red roses playing over and over. I dance until I am cold with sweat, until the room is heaving with bodies, and enlightenment is almost within reach.

When He comes back from the explosion in his Eastern headquarters, he is whispery and half-deaf, thinner than I've ever seen him. Everyone at the Grand Hotel compliments him on his heroic survival. They look away tactfully when food drops from his trembling fork, and when I lean in to dab at his face after he's finished eating.

I would like to make love to Him, to take the years off his body by giving him mine, but he says this is no longer possible. Instead, he sleeps beside me, stomach squeaking and groaning.

The air is thick, and his body gives off a smell like something dying.

In spring, I see things that could be dreams. A train platform in the capital, lumped with people waiting to flee south. A view of pale sky through a cracked ceiling in the chancellery building. A shattering of glass in the wintry courtyard, where the secretaries have been doing target practice. A big metal door and a concrete staircase leading fifty feet underground.

Places that were once safe aren't safe anymore. People that He once trusted are turning into traitors. But our dreams for the future are still dreams, shimmering like gas on the air.

Clothes are spilling out of my wardrobe at the Grand Hotel, a jumble of colours and textures. I fill my valise with silk and satin, tulle and taffeta, polka dots and florals to brighten up the grey underworld where I am heading. He says he doesn't want me coming to the capital in these dangerous times, but I don't listen. I won't let Him be alone among enemies.

I leave the rest of my clothes for my sisters: Gretl, big with Hermann's baby; Ilse, ramrod thin, staying on at the Grand Hotel after I leave. 'Are you sure you know what you're doing?' she asks me. I tell her yes, I know.

It ends on a couch. In an office fifty feet underground, with the last of His officials standing guard outside the door. I sit to his right, leaning against his arm and telling him he's made me the happiest woman in the world. My feet are drawn up under my full skirt, which is black with appliquéd red roses. A ring glints on my fourth finger, a cyanide capsule in my closed fist.

He says it will be quick and painless. A coldness in my mouth. A smell of bitter almonds after I clamp down. A smooth, pretty face for when I enter the next world. I know He doesn't believe in a life after this one, but maybe my belief is enough for the both of us. I lift my face to brush his old lips one last time before this world ends.

There is enlightenment and there is ignorance, so bright and pure that it's almost a virtue. They will say that I knew nothing, Ilse and Papa and everyone else — that I didn't really know Him and that's how I could follow him underground. In a way, they will be right.

We are on a couch together and my eyes are closed before his. We are on a couch together, and then He is standing up while I dress, smiling at my lowered golden head. He is telling me I'm good, but what thrills me is the thought that I'm not. If I look up at his face now, maybe I'll see something terrible.

Martha

There's a tradition here at Sing Sing that the strongest go to the chair last. Strongest how, nobody says, but I'd like to believe it's not only my weight they're talking about. I'd like to believe there's some kind of strength that's been with me always, waiting to be found, like oil at the bottom of an ocean. Strength that wasn't Ray's, though he might've brought it out with his loving.

If I'm honest though, my weight probably has more to do with it. People love what they can measure, and I've got a good forty pounds on Ray.

Most folks think us large women are sexless, old before our time. That just isn't true. Even before Ray, I tried to get it regular, every week if I could. I guess it must have done something to me, having my brother sneak into my room so many nights as a kid; got me used to it early.

I had my share of young men when I was an Army nurse in California. Yankees. Rednecks. Dagos. Sambos. They were all the same, where it mattered; their pimples and peach fuzz, their small dicks they used like weapons. I knew love had no more to do with it than with what happened after Ma turned the lights out, and that I was meant to keep quiet in the same way. But that didn't keep me from laying down in the dark for every service-man who stood in line.

Ernie was one of the few guys who went to the effort of buy-ing me daiquiris beforehand, and he was kind of cute with his squinty black eyes and brows that met in the middle. The days lined up, too, so it made sense to say it was his. He tried denying it. When that didn't work, he jumped off the pier and tried to drown himself. I sat by his bed after they pumped his stomach, watching the rhythms of his chest and stroking his brow, and he looked so lovely I believed he could only have loving words for me when he came to.

Instead, Ernie woke with his face seasick-green and looked at me with the eyes of a drowning man.

'Oh God,' he moaned. 'I wish I was dead.'

Well, I gave Ernie his wish when I moved back to Florida. There's more respectability in being a 200-pound widow than a 200-pound bachelorette and my prospects were better with a ring on my finger — even if it wasn't bought by a man, but out of the settlement his folks gave me to leave him be. I told the neighbours Ernie had been killed in the Pacific and for weeks had them doing my cleaning and bringing over Key lime pies. The local paper even paid me for a story about my tragedy, which called Ernie a 'national hero' and me his 'brave young widow'.

I never heard from Ernie again. I like to think that he really did die soon after, that all those young men did: blasted out of the clouds, eaten by tiger sharks, taken prisoner by the Japs. Somehow, it only seems fair.

Willa Dean was a cute, dark-eyed baby, but sometimes her crying was too much for me. I could almost see where Ma was coming from with her spankings, though I had always told myself I'd do better than that. Most times when it got too much, I'd leave Willa with my across-the-road neighbour Birdie, or if Birdie couldn't take her I'd crush a sleeping pill into her banana puree. That would usually give me a few hours of my own.

With the war over, I picked up a few ex-navy types in the bars of Pensacola, but most of the men were older, like Al. He worked as a bus driver and had a gut and plenty of grey hair, which I figured would make him more likely to stick around than the others, when I started throwing up my morning eggs. To his credit, he did, long enough to give our Anthony a proper name. Sadly, once the christening was over with, so were we.

Al said it was my moods that made him up and leave. It's true, I've had rages so black they've left me blinking up at the ceiling lights. If you ask me though, Al would've left anyway, moods or none.

It was harder being lonesome, knowing what it was to have a man around the house. I was always finding things Al left behind — his belt, his razor, his driving cap — and couldn't bring myself to get rid of them, knowing all I would've been left with were my bonbon wrappers, and my big bras hung over the radiator. Sometimes I thought about using Al's belt or razor on myself.

Other thoughts, too: drowning myself in the bay, putting my head in the oven, sleeping pills. The last way always seemed like the kindest, for me and for the babies. Of course, I would have to take the babies with me; I couldn't die in peace with them crying over me.

What always stopped me was the thought of my own body, lying huge and mottled, waiting to be found. After nursing school, I had worked for a time as a mortician's assistant, so I knew what dying did to a person — the bloating and the rictus and the discolouration. Somehow, it was easier to live with the shame of my body as it was, fat folds and dimples and all, than to die with it.

I've tried all kinds of reducing diets in the past: the Joan Crawford, the grapefruit-and-egg, the Lucky Strike, where you trade sweets for cigarettes. It didn't matter what it was, I always wound up with a flat emptiness inside my belly, a tightness in my jaw that wouldn't go away until I put something in my mouth — and by 'something', I don't mean grapefruit or a Lucky. The few occasions when I did grit my teeth and push through the hunger pains, I ended up blacking out, only coming to when the kids were crying and my pantry eaten bare.

Folks at the hospital used to joke about how I looked, too. 'Avalanche Martha', they'd call me, on account of my white uniform and the way I rushed through those narrow halls. But I got things done and everyone knew it.

Probably if I was a skinny, pretty thing they wouldn't have made me superintendent of the children's ward at twenty-seven.

But, like I said, folks don't think of fat women as being women. Not in the same way as all the pretty little nurses under my charge.

Sure, I was sharp with them sometimes: Shirley and Doris and Thelma and all those other foolish flirts who'd only gone into nursing in hope of catching a doctor. Sometimes I enjoyed reprimanding them on the shortness of their hems and the sheerness of their stockings. Sometimes I got a kick out of making them stay back changing bedpans when they had dates to meet. Sometimes I yelled just to see them jump like Jiminy Cricket.

But that didn't give them the right to play the cruel trick on me that they did.

St. Valentine's Day crept up on me that year from behind, like a prowler in an alleyway. I was coming back from my dinner break when I saw it, sitting in the middle of my desk. It had been torn from the pages of a magazine — the kind full of diet tips and advertisements for beauty products — and circled in bright red. No one walking by could have missed it.

Are you lonely and shy?
Then join Mother Dinene's Family Club for Lonely Hearts!

None of the girls were in sight, and yet I could hear them all laughing, the shrillest sound in the world. I can't say what precisely happened next, but suddenly the ceiling lights were brighter than I remembered and my girls too shook up to even shed a tear. Dr Geyer, our resident paediatrician, clapped his hand on my shoulder then and said it might be best for my nerves if I took the rest of the week off.

~

The last thing I planned was to actually write in to the lonely-hearts club. I hadn't even known I'd kept that scrap of paper, but it kept showing up in the corner of my eye. One night, after putting the kids to bed, I found it peering up at me from the dining table where I was sitting with my pack of Luckys. My eyes watered from the smoke. I stubbed out my cigarette on the magazine page. Then I picked up a pen.

I knew if anyone at the hospital got wind of me advertising for dates, I'd get the can. But I also knew I was nearing thirty, and the bars in Pensacola seemed smaller every week, and my body was crying out for something other than sitting at home alone. I was so dog-tired of being lonesome, I was just about ready to chew my own leg off.

Ray's first letter came that spring, a warm Spanish breeze from grey Manhattan. *This is my first letter for the lonely-hearts club.* Lies. *I live alone in my own apartment, much too large for a lonely bachelor.* Lies. *Why did I choose to write to you? Because you are a nurse, so I know you have a full heart and a great capacity for love and comfort.* Truth, maybe. Ray always had a plum way of mixing his lies up with something like truth.

Even knowing what I know now, that Ray was trying to take me as a fool the same as the rest of them, I wouldn't have done things any differently. I'd still have forked over 99 cents for the finest stationary at Edgerdam's. I'd still have sprayed my perfume over each *billet-doux*, and closed each envelope with a kiss. I'd still have snipped a lock of my hair when he asked for it — dark reddish-brown like dried blood — to do his shady voodoo magic.

Why? Because it made my heart beat faster and still does, thinking back. Because it was high time I was courted for once.

Ray knew more than a thing or two about courting. *Ramón*, as he signed his letters so sweetly. That lilting Spanish way of his came across even on paper, though his English was actually far better than most. His willingness to write about his feelings made him seem so Continental, so unlike American men. That and his photograph — all black hair and burning eyes and a rose in his lapel.

For days after each letter, I'd be walking on air, blushing like a Christmas ham. I'd forget about being hungry and then remember, and take more than usual pleasure in my meals. There was something extra-sweet about unwrapping a bonbon and slipping it into my mouth, with Ray on my mind.

I didn't think of it as lying, not telling about my weight or the kids or those black moods of mine. It was more like a smear of Vaseline over a camera lens, a little something to make the picture more flattering. And if I was edgy about meeting him, when he wrote of making the trip down that summer, it was nothing next to the thumping of my heart.

It's a cruel thing to think back to that sunny day I met Ray at Pensacola Station, and then to think of where we are now. How hopeful it looks from here, like a postcard, the colours saturated and the edges just so slightly water-stained. Birdie had taken the kids overnight and helped me choose a dress — black, slimming, with a gay scalloping of lace around the collar. On top of my curls, I'd pinned a little black hat with a fine birdcage of black net.

I knew him as soon as he stepped onto the platform, by the rose in his lapel and the fedora on his head and his light gentleman's traveling suit, but most of all by his look. A look that took in the whole of me, from my little black hat to the bows on my black pumps, and saw past the fat to the hopeful, well-scrubbed woman that I was.

'Marta.' My name flicked off his tongue like some kind of exotic pebble. Then he gave me the rose.

For Ray's visit, I'd stocked the Frigidaire with all those things men love: sirloin steak, cold cuts, beer, olives, figs, and chocolate pudding. There was also wine, him being European, and scotch, in case he preferred the strong stuff. I'd blown most of my pay cheque on making sure his belly would be filled and his senses dulled, but it turned out I hadn't needed to spend a dime. We were in bed before I even had a chance to put that rose of his in water.

It was loving like I'd never even dreamed. Not a quick, shameful thing in the dark, but birdsong and coins of light through the curtains. Afterward, I fed Ray olives straight out of the jar and he licked the brine from my fingers. He couldn't seem to get enough of me, grabbing handfuls of my flesh and cooing into my ear, 'Marta, Marta, you are so much woman! You'll take care of me, no?'

I'd take care of him. I wanted to shout from the skies that I'd take care of him, that I'd fill his flat belly and give him sponge baths and bring him drinks on ice every day of the week, so long as I could have him in my bed. For kicks, I even put on my uniform for him and played nurse. He had this cute way of flinching every time I brushed the hair from his forehead and tried to mop his brow with the wet cloth.

Things changed the next afternoon when Birdie started banging on my door and bleating, 'Martha! For *shame*. These babies have been crying for you since breakfast!'

It wasn't just Ray's spooked look and the way he covered it up so quickly, or even how sweetly he told me he adored children. Actually, it was the smell in the bedroom that told me I'd been bewitched: brown rose and liquor and brine, all mixed up with our body odours. A smell not so different from all the others who'd shared my bed over those past seventeen years.

I didn't send Ray packing then, nor in the days to come. Instead, I watched him. I watched him with Willa Dean and Anthony, doing a funny trick with his nose and teaching them a ditty about big fat elephants with waving trunks. I watched him when I dropped hints about some money I might have in the bank and where my best jewellery was kept. I watched him when he didn't think I was watching.

If I had diamonds and rubies enough, I'd have hidden them within his eyeshot and let him rob me, bit by bit. As it was, I didn't have much in the world worth stealing and Ray didn't have much cause to stay. Every day, I saw him getting edgier, checking the train timetables when he thought I wasn't looking. One morning, he stepped out to make a phone call while I was cooking his eggs and ham, and returned with his hat in his hands.

'*Marta*, my sweet. Alas, my business needs me back immediately.' His voice was soft, his eyes sadder than an orphan's, his suitcase already packed. 'I will send for you as soon as my affairs permit.'

Try as I did to delay him, to bribe him with promises of fried lunches and pay cheques to come, he was on the express to New York by midday. The kids were home from nursery school, but it only made me lonelier to see them staring at me with the eyes of Al and Ernie. 'Quit your goggling!' I shouted at them, puffing myself up larger than usual, until they both began to snivel. That gave me a moment's satisfaction. Then I started snivelling, too.

I never dreamed of New York City the way some folks do. I guess it always seemed too far from me, like London or Paris or any other city in the world with tall skyscrapers and snow in the winter. But when I arrived there on the morning train with my suitcase and black dress, I liked the way it made me feel. Small, anonymous, strong in my anonymousness. Like my loneliness didn't matter, any more than what I'd eaten for breakfast.

Ray's apartment wasn't big, like he'd told me. Even by New York standards, it seemed pretty mean to me, squeezing in after the Polack superintendent and his belt of keys. 'You wait for Mr Fernandez here,' he said. 'You no interrupt my dominoes again.'

And so I sat myself down on a rickety piano stool and waited. Waited and snooped.

Small as the place was, Ray had plenty of fine things. Cigarette cases, watches, ivory cufflinks, silk ties, and a great many gold finger-rings. There were suits, too, of tailored soft cashmere and wool. What caught my eye most though was his bureau, or what he had stuck up over it — swatches of hair in all colours, from faded blonde to artificial copper to my own dried-blood-red. Every one of them tied with ribbon and speared with pins.

It was a cruel feeling, seeing that, like being ten years old again and flipped onto my belly in the dark. For an instant, I felt weak. Then I was inside those drawers, reading other women's words, the pathetic keening of them like a gate in need of oiling. *Whether tomorrow is bright or blue, there is one lasting thing — my love for you.* Miss Ida Dickinson, Iowa. *Sinse I was a littel girl I have prayd for a man who traits me like a princese.* Miss Loretta Browne, Ohio. *Te quero mucho, Ramon! Me corozone!* Miss Charlotte Putnam, New Hampshire. Words that made me more ashamed to be a woman than all the flesh on my body.

Not remembering all that happened next makes it better in a way. Because it's all still dark to me, from the moment I heard Ray's keys in the door to when I woke up in bed with him. The first thing I noticed when I came to was that I was naked, and then that he was naked. So naked that even the thick black hair of his head was gone, replaced by a bald dome with a crooked white scar across it. 'Now there are no secrets between us, *Marta*,' Ray said slyly, a little sadly. I followed his eyes to the nightstand and saw a toupee lying there like a dead rat. 'No secrets.'

We had some good times in that little apartment of his, in those next few weeks especially. The smallness didn't bother me any, since it meant being closer to him. Every morning, I got to listen to him trickling into the toilet bowl, which was just about the cutest sound I ever heard. I got to toast his breakfast bagels and kiss the crumbs from his lips. I got to bully that superintendent of his about busted pipes and cracks in the plasterwork.

Ray seemed to like having me around too, once he got it into his head that I was there to stay. If you ask me, he enjoyed having someone to talk about his scams with. 'This watch, given to me by lady from Wisconsin. This candelabra, I find in old lady's house in Carolina. This apartment, belonged to widow I married for one month. Also old, very old.' He spoke innocently, like a little boy who snatches eggs from birds' nests. 'All the ladies love me. I give them what they want and then I take. It is fair game.'

Maybe it was fair and maybe it wasn't. I do know that it gave me the willies to see Ray's voodoo, the locks of hair he fashioned into dolls and the love notes he set alight. But when he came to me with smoke on his hands and told me what he saw, my fears flew from me like pigeons from the windowsill.

'*Marta*. I see the little girl with the pretty red curls. She is crying every night. Why does she cry? Why does nobody hear her? I think, yes, my little girl wants to be loved ...'

Helping Ray out with his lonely-hearts scam was my idea. He hadn't wanted a partner, had argued that it was a solo operation. I argued back that it couldn't hurt to have a woman's opinion. Really, it was just that as soon as he started talking about making a trip to Cleveland to fleece some desperate divorcée, I started worrying he'd never come back. If anyone knew how persuasive a desperate woman could be, I did.

So it was that I began sorting through his correspondence, shucking off any prospects that weren't to my liking. If they were too forward with him, for instance, or their portraits too attractive (though Ray claimed the loveliest photographs were always fifteen or twenty years out of date.) Likewise, they couldn't be too savvy. What we looked for were the believers, moony-eyed and superstitious, who wore their bleeding hearts like brooches and their loneliness like too much cheap perfume.

Our first was a farmhouse upstate, belonging to a spinster in her middle fifties. She was a Puritan of some kind so she wouldn't meet Ray without a chaperone, which suited me just fine. Together, we rode up in a rented Pontiac: 'Charles Martin' and his respectable married sister 'Mildred'. We spent two dull nights sitting by a crackling fire drinking apple cider and, in the dead of the third, took off with $300 in bonds and an engraved Civil War pistol.

There were others after that, all over New England and into the Midwest. Best in my eyes were the God-fearing ones, who came away from Ray in a blush but always kept their lips pursed and their drawers on. Sadly, his feelings about them weren't the same as mine.

'These white church bitches, they are stingy. They do not keep nice things and do not trust until we are standing at altar.' Ray kept sighing and rubbing his flat belly. 'Alas, I shall starve, *Marta*.'

Of course he was being dramatic, but I couldn't stand the thought of Ray going without when I'd vowed to take care of him. He deserved the finest in life: caviar, cufflinks, champagne in crystal goblets. And if I couldn't provide it, some other dame surely would.

~

Miss Fay was a Catholic, which meant the breeding instinct was even stronger in her than most. I saw it as soon as we arrived at that poky place of hers in Albany, with all its near-naked Christ figures. But all Ray saw were the dollar signs.

'She will give ten thousand dowry for me to marry her. *Ten thousand!*'

Though close to seventy, the bitch wasn't as frail as all that, and was always cuddling up to Ray on the pretext of showing him her Virgin Mary collection or admiring his fine suits. It got under my skin so much that once, when he was out of the room, I put it into her head that he could do with a haircut.

'No, no, sweetheart! I have trusted barber in New York City! You will see ...' He squirmed as Miss Fay tried to fit a towel around his shoulders, much like I used to imagine Ernie squirming in the hands of the Japs.

Ray didn't show me much loving that week in Albany; not nearly so much as he did the Fay woman, it seemed. Because her hearing was bad, I had the occasion to jump on him a few times when she was saying her prayers or snoring in bed, but mostly Ray gave all his loving to her, and I didn't go crying about it. I sat in the back of the sedan while she rode shotgun with him, driving from bank to bank to draw funds for her dowry. I didn't bite her head off at the dinner table, when she had the nerve to ask him, 'Charles, how is it that you're so nice and lithe, and your sister so stout?' I shared a queen bed with her at night, and never once put a pillow over her face, no matter how many chances I had. I kept my moods in check — until I didn't.

It wasn't my plan to bump her off, any more than it had been Ray's. It's just, when I got up for a midnight snack and saw her side of the bed empty, then heard the hoo-ha in his quarters — well, that did it for me. One minute, I was seeing her old face turned up to his on the pillow, as gleeful as a little girl's. The next minute, the face was no longer gleeful, was hardly a face even, and I was holding something wet and heavy.

'My God, *Marta*,' Ray was whispering, all his warm Latin colour gone. '*Marta*, what have you done …?'

Of all the things that could've gone through my head, cleaning up that night, it was Ray's first letter that I thought of: *Why did I choose to write to you? Because you are a nurse, so I know you have a full heart and a great capacity for love and comfort.* Over and over again, those words, and a thudding determination in me to live up to them. And I did. While he lost his lunch somewhere in the hallway, I took care of the mess, as only a professional could.

We put Miss Fay in the trunk of the sedan. The next morning, we'd skip town, but for those small, dark hours, I wanted only to bring him comfort. It was true, I had a great capacity for it.

The French dame lived in a pretty shingle-style house a little way outside Grand Rapids. She wasn't really French but her name was, and the way she moved around in her low dresses and high-waist slacks, smoking in drawback, you'd think she was in a foreign film or something. She had a baby daughter, too, also with a French name, and just about the most pampered thing you ever saw in her smocked dresses and ringlets that smelled of strawberry shampoo. Thinking back to Willa Dean and Anthony where I'd last left them, crying on the stoop of the Salvation Army Church, it seemed a crime for any child to be so cared for.

Since Miss Fay, we'd been living out of our suitcases. Her dowry kept us in milk and honey, but we never talked about settling down. After what had happened, I couldn't help feeling a sunny lawn in the suburbs was out of bounds.

Ray seemed to feel it, too, with a kind of spooked pride. 'You love me so much,' he'd say. 'I know it. You are so much woman.'

But woman as I was, that didn't stop him goggling at Frenchy.

Delphine was what she called herself — French for 'dolphin', which was pretty stupid, if you ask me. She was a young forty-one, not fifty pretending to be forty like a lot of those others. She had loved her husband very much, but he 'was never the same after the war' and had died 'tragically' soon after little Rainelle was born. She didn't trust the men who came courting when Mr Downing was barely cold in the ground. Her dream was to find a 'man of character', interested in a 'lasting commitment'.

'I hope you understand,' she told Ray. 'I have a little girl to think of.'

For all her talk, it only took the bitch a couple of days to open up her bedroom to Ray. There was nothing I could do about it either. She wasn't deaf like the other one and when I tried to put my hands under Ray's clothes or give him little smooches, he'd just say, '*Marta*, control yourself! There is baby present.'

That baby. Why he gave a damn what happened to her I don't know, when he never once mentioned Willa Dean and Anthony.

Maybe he sensed what a ticking time bomb little Rainelle was. Though happy enough to toddle off with me for an ice-cream cone or taffy in the playground, the sight of Ray almost always had her in tears. If he happened to be touching or even seated near her mama, she'd start wailing, 'Maaa! Maaa!' and not even that ditty about the fat elephants and their wavy trunks could calm her.

Ray didn't like to leave us dames alone together, but most days we'd be waiting at least a half-hour for him to finish grooming himself. 'I've never known a man to spend so long in the bath,' Delphine gushed one morning, too dreamy to even touch the tower of pancakes she'd just made. She actually seemed to think we were friends, funnily enough; that me taking her kid to the park while she rolled around with Ray made us something like sisters-in-law.

'Oh, Charles has always been that way,' I sneered. 'A real dandy.'

Delphine didn't even bat an eye; she was too dumb or too in love, I guess. Instead, she rested her chin on her hand and mistily stared at the planters on the windowsill. 'That lovely thick hair …' she sighed. Then she started fussing about his coffee getting cold, saying maybe she should make a fresh pot, and it was such a pathetic thing that it would've been a crack-up, if she hadn't kept going on and on. So I said it, just to shut her up.

'Why don't you surprise him, Dolphin? Take it to him in the bath …?'

Seeing Delphine scuttling around, getting the new pot ready, gave me a mean kind of satisfaction. Little Rainelle sat in her highchair, following her mama with round saucer-eyes. Hardly a minute later, there was a crash in the bathroom and the scream-ing started. Ray came running out after Delphine, stark naked except for the toupee he was fixing over his scar, and he was pleading, 'Darling, darling, it's me, Charles! I am the same man! Don't be crazy, please!'

But she was already sobbing and taking Rainelle into her arms, who of course was in a state by that point, with Ray so close and naked to boot. He had managed to replace his toupee and with his free hands was grabbing at Delphine — her wrists, her hair, the belt of her dressing gown. It was a hell of a scene, like something out of a potboiler. I even stopped eating my pan-cakes for a better view, just in time to see Ray getting an elbow to the face and mama and baby rushing to the door.

'Bitch!' He put his hand to his nose. For the first time, he noticed me watching. 'Fat bitch! What are you playing at? Help me!'

I remember he looked so puny standing there, his toupee on askew and his lovely long dick hiding inside itself. Not at all like the spell-caster who could turn broken hearts into gold.

Even though I'd been ready to do in my Willa Dean and Anthony at one stage, dealing with Rainelle made me glad I'd never had to. You wouldn't think it, but it was more of a struggle in some ways with the bawling and the frog-kicking and the little face turning blue. Then again, maybe working on the children's ward prepared me somewhat for the last part. We were always having little ones coming in near-purple with the croup and so forth.

Ray and I went to a matinee afterward. *When My Baby Smiles At Me*. Everyone likes going to the movies when they're in need of cheering up and we were no different. It was nice, too, sitting there in the dark with a big bucket of popcorn between us. Ray had left his toupee at the house, figuring it was time for a change anyhow, and in the middle of the film he sweetly laid his bare head on my breast. By the time we got out, I think we'd both near forgotten the cleaning up that was waiting for us back at Delphine's. The streetlights were so bright it was like coming from a blackout.

There's no death penalty in Michigan, which is why they extradited us to New York State. It was a cruel trick to pull, but I guess it was fool of us to trust a bunch of men with our lives, and lawmen at that. As we were boarding the metal bird, the marshals kept joking about what a risk it was flying with such heavy cargo. Which just proves my point about folks only caring about what they can measure.

It was shaky up in the air, but we had a nice view of all the lakes and scudding clouds. Honestly, I wouldn't have minded going down then. For one thing, it would've saved us the trouble of the trial. For another, I wouldn't have had to worry about my body, what kind of spectacle it was going to make.

Because that's the one thing everyone wants to talk about: my body. How much it weighs, how Ray could've ever put his hands on it, how much voltage it will take to kill.

I've been thinking about it, too — about what's going to happen when they pull that switch. I like to believe there isn't voltage enough in the world to put me out, that even if all the lights of New York City go into that surge, my heart will still be thud-thudding with love for Ray. Because some things in this world have to be beyond measuring.

Caril

Charlie waits for me outside the school gates, leaning against his Ford and smoking Camels. Charlie's cooler than anyone I know. He wears a black windbreaker and has his hair done real high and slick. I run to him as soon as the bell rings and let him kiss me right there against the car for everyone to see. I don't care what the girls in my class say. None of them have a boyfriend as cool as Charlie, who's been out of school for years and doesn't have to earn his wages on some dumb old farm.

My momma says that Charlie is trash. No better than the garbage bags he hauls from sun-up till ten a.m. She doesn't care that he scrubs himself up real good before meeting me, so I can barely smell the garbage. He pays for all our dates and buys me presents whenever he can afford to — gumballs, hair barrettes, even a plush white kitten.

I'm failing math and I might be held back a year, if I'm not careful. But no matter how hard I try, I can't get myself to concentrate on the fuzzy chalk numbers on the blackboard, the books full of boring words. When I bring home Ds to my momma and stepdaddy, they scream at me until baby Betty Jean starts screaming, too. 'It's that Starkweather kid, isn't it? That boy's trash. One of these days, he's gonna knock you up, and you'll be out on your ass!'

Charlie never liked school either. The boys at Lincoln High used to call him names — Lil Red, Bandy Legs, Peckerhead — and make fun of the way he talked. In gym class, he'd get back at them by throwing balls at their heads, or tackling them to the ground when they weren't looking. He's always happy when he tells me how badly he hurt those boys, many of them bigger and stronger, and I'm happy for him. I tell him, 'Good on you, Chuck. They deserved it.'

In the Ford, Charlie guides my hand on the gearstick. I bump along with him through muddy paddocks, squealing as the windows are spattered with dirt and cow shit. 'You're doin' good, baby,' he says in my ear. 'You're drivin'.' My hands are firm on the wheel. All around us, cows are lowing. Grey geese gather in the sky like clouds in tornado season.

I'm fourteen now and gaining flesh. Hips that weren't there before and fat, pale breasts I try to hide under my loosest shirts. I feel like a cow, but Charlie says I've never looked prettier. He takes me to the Runza Drive Inn for ground-beef rolls that leave my hands greasy and my clothes covered in pastry flakes. When I get home, I try hard to eat up Momma's cooking, but it's not easy with my stepdaddy grumbling across the table. 'I'll be damned if that girl isn't knocked up. Look at all the pounds she's packing.'

Charlie says he wants to marry me. Around town, he's been spreading the word about how we're going to live together, all the babies he's going to put inside me. I tell him he shouldn't be saying such stupid things, but he says it's a compliment and, besides, I shouldn't be calling him stupid. So I let him run his mouth, figuring it's easier than trying to shut him up.

We're still flushed from driving, looking out at the frozen cornfields, when Charlie says he's got something to show me. I wonder if maybe he's going to get his gun and shoot a goose from the sky, like he did one time. Instead, he jumps down from the hood of the Ford and fumbles in his windbreaker for a little gold ring.

'Caril, baby, let's do this. Let's get h-hitched.'

The wind is in his hair, picking up the bright red tufts. I've always found Charlie's red hair pretty, like his green cat eyes, but right now I'm finding it hard to look at him.

'I can't, Chuck,' I tell him. My tongue feels heavy and cold, like I've been sucking on icicles. 'Not while I'm still in school. Momma would never let me.'

'Damn your momma! Come on. D-don't you want to wear it?'

He starts trying to put the ring on my finger. It's cold, and his hands are so rough they make me pull away. '*No*,' I say, and my voice sounds meaner than I want, but sometimes it's hard getting Charlie to understand any other way.

Something flickers in Charlie's eyes and he shoves the ring back in his pocket. Then, sooner than I can slip off the car's hood, he's kicking at the fender, cussing the whole world and me.

'Goddammit! Damn you! If you only knew what I goed through to get this shitty ring ...'

Charlie hasn't come to get me from school since our blowout so I've been taking the big yellow bus. It's slow and full of stupid boys from my class, who aren't anywhere near as nice as Charlie. It makes me think maybe I was too hard on him and should call him up when I get home. Only after I've done my homework though. Things have been better since I've been doing my homework, and my stepdaddy's even saying I could make something of myself someday, like a nurse or a kindergarten teacher.

The house is quiet and after I've opened the screen door, it flies shut behind me with a crash. And just like that, Charlie is standing in the doorway with his .22 rifle pointed at me, yelling, 'Go in and sit down!'

'Chuck?' I look from the gun barrel to his freckled face, and think it must be some kind of joke, though my heart is racing like a rabbit's. 'Don't be stupid. Put that down.'

'I tolded you, sit!' he yells again. Then: 'Don't you ever call me s-stupid.'

So I go into the den and to Momma's rocking chair, the one she likes to sit in with Betty Jean. I start asking Charlie where everyone is, but he won't answer, just keeps pacing around with his rifle, tilting his head every now and again like he's hearing something I can't. After a while, I start crying, and he says, 'They ain't here, okay! I tolded them it's just you and me from now on.' Then he switches on the TV.

We watch a lot of TV that night, so much my head hurts and

my eyes get small and squinty. The only time Charlie lets me get up is to fix us some dinner and once to use the bathroom, and he follows me like a shadow.

'I can't go with you watching,' I tell him, when he wants me to leave the door open. He just laughs and says I must think I'm pretty special, and do I really think he's never seen water before. Since I don't have much choice either way, I unbutton my jeans and settle over the bowl, tugging down my shirt so he can't see between my legs. Even then, all I can manage is a trickle.

The next morning, I'm waking up sore in my momma's bed. Outside, the world is dull and frozen: frost-covered chicken coop, frost-covered yard, frost-covered scrap metal. In the kitchen, Charlie's frying eggs and crooning like Elvis on an off day, his red hair slick with my stepdaddy's pomade. I hug my body and ask if he's going to drive me to school. 'Course not, baby. You don't ever have to go back to that dump.'

Come afternoon, the neighbours are knocking to be let in. Charlie turns down the TV and tells me to get rid of them. So I button my housecoat real tight and tiptoe to the front door, scowling through the screen. 'You can't come in. Betty Jean's got a real bad flu. It's con-tay-jus.'

Afterward, Charlie gives me a pen and paper and tells me to make like I'm writing a note from my mother. *Stay a way Every body is sick with the Flue*, I copy out in my neatest handwriting. Charlie says it looks swell and tapes it to the door. Then he goes around and makes sure all the doors and windows are locked and all the curtains drawn shut.

For a whole week, I don't change out of my housecoat. The TV is on all day, so we see all the programs, from the baby shows in the morning to the talk shows late at night. Charlie drives into town for groceries and comes back with bags of potato chips, a tub of ice-cream, and three big bottles of Pepsi, which we drink with every meal. 'Ain't this romantic? Like a honeymoon,' he says again and again. We neck sometimes, but it isn't much fun with no one around to tell us off, and Charlie always wants to take things further.

Once a day, Charlie goes into the backyard to feed the chickens and look inside the outhouse. He doesn't tell me why, but near the end of the week, he says, 'Boy, it stinks in there.'

I believe Charlie when he says it's time to split, though I don't know whether I'll ever see my momma, stepdaddy, or baby Betty Jean again. I tie one of Momma's scarves up under my chin and pocket her lipstick, telling myself that it's only to borrow; that I'll be back as soon as the ice has melted and Charlie has stopped acting so crazy.

Charlie drives us over to Old Man Meyer's farm. Old Man Meyer has lots of guns. He has known Charlie since he was a little boy. It was Old Man Meyer who taught Charlie to shoot and skin jackrabbits. 'I'm the best shot that old man's ever seen,' Charlie brags to me. 'And he's seen a lotta shooting.'

When Charlie pulls up on the muddy track outside Old Man Meyer's farmhouse, the dog is barking. The old man is hobbling out in his overalls, waving a .410 shotgun. 'Hey, M-mister Meyer!' Charlie calls out. 'It's just me and Caril. Can you lend us some ammo?'

I wave at the old man and he stops squinting to smile at me. 'Pretty Caril Ann! What are you doing going around with this jackass ...?'

Old Man Meyer's bedroom smells of wool and tobacco. I'm wiping my eyes with his nubby blanket as Charlie tries on hats, doffing and swaggering in the looking glass. 'That was a rotten thing to do, Chuck! Why'd you have to go and pull your gun on Mister Meyer?' Charlie tosses his hat on the bed and grumbles, 'I didn't like the way he was l-looking at you, not one bit.'

Charlie fills his pockets with bullets and spare cash. He gives me the .410 to keep, telling me I'll need something to protect myself. In the kitchen, we make a meal of the rabbit stew bubbling on Old Man Meyer's stovetop. 'We'll stay here, just for tonight,' Charlie says.

The wind is pounding and the dog is crying in my dreams. Charlie's stumbling out naked into the cold, unloading his rifle at the whining, wagging darkness. 'Now we can get us some sleep,' he says. He cuddles up behind me, cold-skinned. His hardness is like a gun muzzle against my spine.

The shotgun is heavy against my shoulder, trudging through the mud in my white boots. 'Why'd you have to go get the car stuck, Chuck?' I ask him again.

'Aw, baby, you know I didn't mean to.'

The sky turns dark early at this time of year and the bare trees are scary, bent and blackened like witches on a stake. I think of how scary the old man's body looked and feel like I'm about to cry, but Charlie's watching me closely. Then a car winds into sight, and Charlie nudges me. 'Look here, Caril. Stick out your thumb.'

We're rugged up, riding back into town with two preppy kids, who laugh when they see our rifles and ask if we've been out hunting. 'Yeah, something like that,' Charlie says. The prep boy has glasses and talks like he's thirty years old, not seventeen. His girl is pretty. She has dark hair like mine and her name is like mine: Carol, spelled the proper way. I see the girl looking at Charlie and get a funny feeling, like a cold skin of ice over my stomach.

I wait in the car as Charlie leads the prep kids down the abandoned tornado shelter. The windows are rolled up and the winds are whirring enough for me to convince myself I don't hear the shots. Charlie's gone awful long and is wiping off his hunting knife when he climbs out of the shelter, jeans unbuckled. His red hair is snow-specked and tossed from the wind. 'It's too damn cold,' he mutters. 'Too damn cold.'

We're curled up together inside the locked car, on the rich side of town. Charlie is watching the sunrise, squinting at the mansions from behind the glasses he swiped from that prep boy. 'I used to haul trash here,' his words edge into my sleep. 'You wouldn't believe the stuff these rich folks throwed out.' A man in a long wool coat and fedora leaves one of the mansions, suitcase in hand, and gets into a shiny black Packard. I yawn as I watch the man drive off and Charlie load his rifle. 'Let's get us some breakfast, baby,' he says.

The maid is wailing as she tries to cook us pancakes, slopping mixture and dropping a whisk on the kitchen floor. Opposite me, the rich man's wife sits with her hands tied to the chair back. She wears something long, white, and floaty like a swan's feathers. She smells of everything we don't: soft beds, clean towels, hot showers. 'We want coffee, too,' Charlie is telling the maid, mouthing the words since she's deaf or foreign or something. I look at the rich man's wife and try to make conversation.

'Gee, your dress is real pretty. I wish I could wear something like that to sleep.'

I'm hunched up on the divan in the rich man's library, watching the grandfather clock that hasn't chimed yet, the statue on the mantle of some dead guy with eyes like a catfish. When I hear Charlie's footsteps on the staircase, I look over and see he's shedding his bloody shirt. He's blacked his hair with shoe polish and has an armload of clean clothes.

'Put this on,' he tells me, holding out a light suede jacket.

I look at it. Clean as it is, I shake my head.

'Go on, wear it.'

'I don't want to.'

'Goddammit, Caril!' Charlie takes a step toward me.

I look at the ceiling, then the statue of the dead guy. I swap my dirty blue coat for the clean suede one. When my hands are curled inside the pockets, I ask, 'Can we go now, Chuck?'

'Naw, baby. Not yet.' Charlie throws the pile of clothes on the divan. 'We still gotta get that big shiny car.'

~

We're skipping town in the rich man's Packard. I watch the black road fly ahead of us, the snow and stars falling onto the windshield. Charlie's talking, but listening to him feels like being in school, the way he says the same things over and over. 'People are no good. You're the b-best thing in my life, baby. Don't you wish we were the only two people on earth?'

We're crossing the border and I can see the lights of Cheyenne, but Charlie doesn't want to go anywhere near them. He's talking about driving to Washington State, the two of us living in a cabin in the woods. He keeps talking and I close my eyes, feel my head growing dark and heavy with everything I don't understand.

I wake up to pink skies, slowing. Charlie's pulling up behind a parked Buick on a roadside outside Douglas, Wyoming. Gun over shoulder, he's stepping out of the Packard. I see him knocking on the window of the Buick. I see him jerking his thumb. There's a newspaper on our dashboard with a picture of me and Charlie on the front, a list of all the things we're supposed to have done. I see Charlie pointing his rifle at the Buick and plug my ears, screw shut my eyes. I can hear baby Betty Jean wailing, the dog in the night. A siren starts to whine.

The papers say that Charlie's been sentenced to death. They say that Charlie wants me sitting on his lap when he goes to the chair, frying with him. They print photographs of me looking grownup and snooty, with my new clothes and spit curls. The papers call me a femme fatale, and Charlie tries out the words on the witness stand. 'Caril, she's a real f-f-fem fatal. She made me kill those people. I never met a girl so trigger-happy.'

On the night of Charlie's frying, I watch the clock. I watch the minutes click by as they strap his arms to the chair and fix the metal bowl over his head. I look out at the darkened prison yard, my forehead cold against the window grating. The minute hand ticks one after midnight. I close my eyes and smell the smoke of him on the night air.

They tell me that I'm here for life, but no one knows how long a life is. Some are short like Betty Jean's. Some are long like Old Man Meyer's. If I'm good, they tell me, I might get out sooner, but I shouldn't expect to see the sun while I'm still young and pretty. I shouldn't expect to see the same world when I get out; times are changing and people are getting meaner. Keep your head down, they tell me. Read your books like you've been told. Don't look for freedom on the open road.

Myra

I never doubted how powerful the darkness was, even as a child, lying awake under my tartan quilts and praying for it to end. Those were years when the air raids were still fresh in our minds — stories of the London Blitz and towns turned to rubble overnight. I daresay those stories were what kept me up, listening to the winds rushing from the moor and picturing all of Gorton in ruins come morning. Though the war was over long before my first communion, those early years were enough to convince me that the darkness was not only a real thing, but greater than prayer. Greater than God.

I was a child afraid of the dark. Yet I was also a believer, and what I saw in the night hours of my belief was too powerful to look away from. Rows and rows of identical red-brick houses razed to the ground. Taverns, factories, churches — all razed. On the air, a thickness of dust and smoke that seemed almost magical, like a fairytale.

And us, the children. Led by white hands into that unknown waste.

~

It took Ian one date to convince me that there was no God. In a dark corner of the Thatched House tavern, he drove his words into me like nails.

'It's all *shite*. Religion, God, Good, Evil — superstitious shite. Ordinary people are weak, mindless bloody bovines. Most of them would sooner sleepwalk through life than confront their natural inclinations.'

Weak and *ordinary*. It was as if he had looked into my heart and made out the two things I least wanted to be. Weak and ordinary meant a life of steaming peas and watching *Coronation Street*. It meant marrying some chap who worked in a factory and waiting around in a housecoat for a screaming match and a black eye. It meant church and children and losing all one's money in the pools.

I thrust my chin forward and looked Ian square in the eye. I felt I knew what he meant by 'natural inclinations', but I wanted it from his own lips.

'Nature is primarily sexual,' he said, without a trace of embarrassment. 'In the sense that all creation and destruction is sexual, a violent release of energy.'

'And how do *you* know so much about nature?' I pouted and smoothed my hair, newly dyed a blitzkrieg blonde. I had not yet read the books that Ian had read. I had never heard anyone speak so frankly about such things. The weapons I had at my disposal were few and inferior.

'I spent a year at Strangeways. Another year at borstal. Where there is Crime, there is Nature.'

Ian had a way of pronouncing certain words as if they had a capital letter. To me, this seemed utterly learned and original. There he was, sat right in front of me, this man who I worked with and had loved for a year; a man in white shirtsleeves and braces, with clean fingernails and a low Glaswegian accent; the most unique man I had ever met. Though he wasn't the only chap in Gorton with a criminal record, I doubted any of the others could have spoken about it so intelligently.

'Why were you at borstal?' I wanted to know.

'Does it matter?' Ian sneered. 'My real crime was being born working class and choosing not to work.'

'But you work now.'

'I *choose* to.' A rare smile crossed his handsome features. Dark lashes, dark-blue eyes, pale skin, clean shave. How did a man get so *clean?* 'And I may choose to stop at any time.'

I would have liked to take his face in my hands and kiss him roughly, right then. I chose not to. I've always prided myself on my ability to avoid looking weak. With the others, this had meant resisting advances; with Ian, this meant not making any. Until he walked me back to Gran's house on Bannock Street, at least.

Though he did not take my hand, I became aware of a change in him after we left the tavern. He seemed somehow smaller, walking beside me, his jaw set firmly as if against nerves. *He is weak*, I told myself. *He is not a man.* I listened to the scuff of our shoes against the wet cobbles. I felt the same blend of attraction and repulsion that sometimes came over me at the office when he acted particularly uncouth — insulting me, deliberately walking in front of me, rowing and swearing if he lost in the pools. *A man would not be so cowardly.*

In the shadows of the porch, I saw his pale Adam's apple twitching. He was not looking at me, simply staring across the street and fidgeting with something in the pocket of his dark overcoat — his lock-back knife, I later learned; he carried it everywhere. I wanted him and hated him so intensely it almost blinded me. Taking a step closer, I breathed a stream of vapour. Then I sank my teeth into his ripe lower lip. Hard.

We became lovers that night on the old green settee in Gran's front room. For all his earlier talk, I sensed from his movements that he was as inexperienced as I was — with women, at any rate. More than once, he brushed against my backside and had to be guided forward. I kept on my girdle and my cardigan. He kept on everything save his shoes and his coat. At the end of it, he looked as clean as ever, though rather wan.

Ian hated all religion, but particularly Catholicism, which was the most superstitious in his eyes. I was baptised at St. Francis Monastery and had loved reading about the woman saints as a lass: Joan of Arc, Catherine of Alexandria, Agnes of Rome. On Christmas Eve, Ian and I walked out past the lighted monastery as the bells were tolling for midnight service. I grabbed onto his sleeve without meaning to. The sound, the light, being there with him — that was all.

'Christ is born,' he said. 'Should we kill him in the cradle and get it over with?'

The bells stopped. A deep, low hum of organ music started up from within, visceral.

'Let's go in,' I said. 'Just for a while.'

His face took on that look of disgust that was so already familiar to me — and yet, not quite so familiar that I understood how earnest it was. 'I *refuse* to go into a Catholic church,' he said.

'Come on.' I pulled his sleeve. 'I know you don't believe in it, but it's beautiful on Christmas Eve.'

'Little Myra wants to smell the frankincense, how *sweet*,' Ian jeered. I was not 'little', and that made it worse; the contemptuous way he scanned my breasts and hips as he said it. 'Does she want to lie in a stinking barn, too? Give birth to the Immaculate Conception?'

At that, he pulled his sleeve from my grip and stalked to the plot of graves at edge of the churchyard. I heard him unzip. I saw, rather than heard, the stream of urine he released onto one of the gravestones. He zipped up and looked over his shoulder.

'That's what I think of your church.'

As I went downhill to meet him, I could hear the opening prayer: *Through the night hours of the darkened earth, we the people watch for the coming of your promised son.* Perhaps I ought to have turned back then, but the people seemed so easily profaned next to the two of us.

I am a tender person, more tender than most. Those who know what I've done may argue otherwise, but the fact remains: none of it could have happened if it wasn't for tenderness, Ian's and mine.

He was tender. I saw this from the beginning, along with

everything else — the arrogance, the cruelty, the untouchable cleanness. It drove me to distraction how tender he was. Looking at his soft lips and fresh complexion seemed to turn on something predatory in me, a desire for possession that had always existed, below the fear and the piety and the deadly routine. He was the quarry, I the hunter. I wanted his tenderness, by any means and at any cost.

Through that first winter together, I was little more than Ian's Saturday-night stand. During the week, he was content to sit away from me, eating his egg-and-cheese butties and reading his foreign books. If I approached him and asked something about his reading, he was always polite, but never prolonged our conversations. Many times, I fantasised about ripping the book from his hands and telling him what a right arrogant prick he was. Instead, I asked him to lend me things.

He started me on the Romantic poets: Blake, Wordsworth, Shelley. After that was *Crime and Punishment*. The dirty books — de Sade, Krafft-Ebing, Havelock Ellis — didn't come until later, when he was certain that I would be receptive. There was an order to everything Ian did.

Like the way he would wait until the last minute on Friday afternoon to ask me out. Or the strict pattern our dates followed: a film, the tavern, and Gran's house to make love. If Gran was still up, Ian would stay and take tea with us until she retired, politely talking about the wartime and how there were too many immigrants.

After the first few weeks of shagging the normal way, I let him put it back there. He was so frantic and insistent about it that I just gave in, thinking it would only be that once. The whole act made me feel about as sensuous as a piece of plumbing, but the alcohol helped. Ian and I always had to drink a lot, to do the things we did together.

Things changed in the spring when Ian bought his motorcycle. It was a Triumph Tiger Cub, all black and chrome and hardly bigger than a scooter. He called around at Bannock Street the day that he got it, with a crash helmet tucked under his arm. It was the first time he had ever called on a weeknight.

'Come for a ride,' he said. A statement, not a question.

Though I was already in my rollers and headscarf, I stepped into the humid evening and let him lead me to the bike. He sat down and fitted on his helmet, smirking, 'I don't have one for *you*.' I had a brief image of the bike going down, my blonde head rolling along the roadside. Yet I was completely calm as I settled behind him and clutched his trim waist. If I was going down, I could be certain that he was going with me.

We puttered out of Bannock Street, slow and low to the ground. I could see Gran peering out of the top window, some neighbourhood lasses watching from the corner — friends of my sister, who dated the same gits she did and squealed over the same Beatles records. As we gained speed, I clenched Ian's waist tighter, bracing against the vibrations, rejoicing as those familiar red bricks blurred before my eyes.

Although we did not stop at the moor that day, the sound of it, the smell of it, the sprawl of it, loomed within us both. It was too dark to see the heather that was beginning to bloom, yet I clung to the sweetness of it on the air, the heavy odour of the peat beneath. I felt my scarf slipping in the wind and pressed my chin against Ian's shoulder, thanking our non-existent God that he couldn't see my eyes watering. He had made my world so large, I couldn't help mourning the loss of the smaller one I knew I was leaving behind.

Later, much later, Ian told me his theory about the moor, why it owned both of our souls the way it did. Before we brought any children there, even before we talked about it, we were one with the place, as if our own true forms resided in the peat, the rocks, the soughing wind. I told Ian about the nights I'd lain awake, believing in the darkness more than I believed in God. He told me he had felt something similar as a lad. Then he explained:

'We are demon folk. We don't belong in the mundane world of ordinary people. There's a chasm that separates us from the rest of society. That's why we're drawn to darkness.'

It was a beautiful summer's day, everything blooming and lit up like a fairground: broom, gorse, heather, harebells, sweet smells of honey, pollen, and the German wine we were drinking. Yet, when he gestured at the scenery, I knew exactly what he meant. The ghostly moths floating up from the earth, the clouds strobing above us — a brooding quality, as if it could all switch from light to dark in an instant.

'This is our domain,' he said. 'Everything is permitted here.'

Another might have looked at the sublime landscape and seen proof of God's existence. For Ian, it was the opposite. Standing among the rocks in his tailored grey suit, not a single strand of his dark quiff out of place, he was right in his element. Because of that, I believed him. Also, because I loved him.

The first three murders — Pauline, John, and Keith — happened so smoothly, I believe, because they happened in our domain. Killing on one's own territory is different to killing on common ground. Ancient people knew that. Wild animals know it. Ian did, too. He chose to bring the last two back to the red-brick house, and that was his mistake.

In our quest for new sensations, we become ever more reckless, he wrote to me, sometime after our arrest. It's years now since he and I stopped writing to one another.

From the beginning, there was a tension between how much I knew about Ian and how much I didn't. I knew that he lived with his mother, that he liked German marching music and thought Hitler a genius, that his favourite program was *The Goon Show* and his favourite cigarettes were French. He enjoyed oriental restaurants but hated the people that ran them. He despised Jews but had his suits tailored by a man called Menken. He railed against the proles and the aristocracy in equal measure. He admired the spontaneity and innocence of children but could read passages about their torture and murder with a gentle smile on his lips.

I knew so much, yet in the middle of it all was a centre as cloudy and tumultuous as the moor itself. If he didn't want to see me, he wouldn't, and that was that, no matter what plans we had. If he didn't want to tell me where he'd been, he wouldn't, regardless of the explanations I felt he owed me.

There were nights, pacing around in wait for him, when I was torn between fearing for his life and wishing him dead. Stubbing out fag after fag, I conjured violent scenarios: Ian's bike mangled in a ditch, Ian walking into the path of a speeding bus, Ian getting clobbered by some brute with dirt under his nails and lager on his breath. The satisfaction I gained from these scenarios was almost equal to a tender word from him.

'There's a pub on Canal Street. I like to go there to people-watch,' he said one day, in response to my latest grilling. I knew exactly what kind of place Canal Street was: only men, and only of a particular kind, frequented the pubs there. I gave him a look of disgust and he smiled feebly. Yet that was the last I asked about his activities for some time.

When I first fell in love with Ian, I used to fantasise about having all the ordinary things with him: marriage, children, a nice home. They were bland fantasies, born of wallpaper and furniture catalogues, and I abandoned them soon after we came together. At one point, perhaps a month after we killed Lesley Ann, I believed myself pregnant, and was ill at the thought. The blood that came a few days later seemed to me to be an act of will more than an act of nature.

Though we spoke to no one about our relationship, people saw us together and made their assumptions. He was never publicly affectionate toward me, yet he accepted my presence; in some ways he seemed to depend on it. It was I who purchased tickets, ordered drinks, and placed bets when we were out together. I took care of practicalities, while he sat by with his arms crossed and a right surly look, waiting for his change.

People saw us together and made their assumptions, but they could not have guessed the half of it. My skirts became shorter, my boots taller, my stride broader, my vocabulary rich. I was strong and posh and sexy, in no way ordinary. That was the woman I became with him.

We talked about it so much — the perfect murder. At first, it was in purely theoretical terms: what Raskolnikov sought when he brought down the axe on his landlady's head; where Leopold and Loeb went wrong. Ian loved the story of Leopold and Loeb; so wealthy and dapper and freethinking, yet daft enough to leave a pair of custom-made glasses at the crime scene. He was certain he'd never make such a mistake, that he would be able to account for every button and stitch. After all, his official title at work was 'stock clerk'.

That it should be a child was something he had no trouble justifying. Not only was the act of killing a child more reprehensible to the ordinary human conscience — and thus more thrilling to him — but a child would put up less of a fight.

We talked so much, Ian and I, and suddenly it was our second summer together. I was twenty-one years old and had assimilated the ideas in his filthy books, as I had assimilated everything else about him. I had a driver's license and a van, which I took out to the moor alone some nights, reliving in my mind the times we had spent there together. I didn't fear the night or the winds. I didn't fear anything.

~

Pauline was a friend of my sister. She was an ordinary girl, only five years my junior, quiet and pretty and trusting; I used to babysit for the family when I was in school, and they never gave me any trouble. I had nothing against her, but I had nothing for her either, as I had nothing for any of the people who lived their small lives a world apart from Ian's and mine. Besides, I thought it better a lass of sixteen than a wee babyish thing like he wanted.

I drove the van and he tailed on his motorcycle, shining his headlights when she came into view. She wore pale clothes and looked hardly real against the dusty amber sky, more ghost than flesh and blood. A clockwork ghost of a girl, on her way to a disco to dance with other girls and boys just like her. That made it easier: pulling over, asking if she wanted a lift, all of it.

Less easy was seeing what Ian had done to her. I was not there during the doing, though he might argue otherwise. With my own eyes, I watched the sky through the windshield darkening like a stain. I heard the wind, I smelled the peat, I smoked the last of my Embassy Tipped, and I regret that no one was there to see my hands trembling. Then he rapped on the window and brought me out to look at the pale body on the cotton grass, the pale bunched clothes and dark gurgling wound where her throat had been. He told me she had fought too hard. I asked if he had raped her. 'Of course I did,' he sneered. 'Why wouldn't I?'

The sex was better in the days following the murders. It was real man-woman sex, loving and brutal in equal measure. He was tender with me, too; so tender I felt I could weep. And yet, part of me saw his trembling, the flush on his pale cheeks, and wanted nothing of it.

I began seeing Norman a month or so after Pauline. He was taller and handsomer than Ian, and a police officer — a fact that strangely reassured me. We had met when he saw me parking my van, and I saw right away the ring on his finger, and also that he was very handsome. His jaw was strong and square, and his chin had a dimple in it. Nothing like Ian, whose chin was weak.

Because he was married, we would meet in secret and shag when he was off-duty. Norman liked that I wasn't soft or clinging, that I didn't press for anything more. He liked the interest I showed in his gun and taught me things — how to load and grip, and basic ballistics. He smoothed his big hands over my strong legs and said I would make a good officer, went so far as to bring me pamphlets from the force. When Ian saw them, he laughed and said I ought to try out.

'That *would* be a thrill. And you'll pick up a lot of useful information.'

That set my mind against it, against Norman. Without even trying, Ian had made it all about him again.

I started going to the pistol club soon after Norman. Because of his borstal record, Ian could never visit himself, but he approved of my going and started looking at guns for us to buy. He wanted a Luger, of course, like the German soldiers used. In the end, we settled for British guns: a Webley .45 and a Manchester-made target rifle.

On the moors, we shot wild sheep. Ian joked that Jews would have made better target practice, but the sheep were practically the only creatures that ventured into our domain. I came to enjoy seeing them fall, their daft bleats and their woolly bodies dropping onto the heath. We did nothing with the carcasses, no burials or desecration, though sometimes we'd observe them weeks afterward, rotting slowly in the cold air. If they happened to fall on peat soil, they rotted more slowly still. It was good science, seeing that.

I became a fair shooter with practice, though not as accurate as Ian. I was always what they call 'trigger-happy', wont to fire before I had my aim right. He tried to train this out of me but never completely succeeded, and part of him seemed to think it was a good thing anyhow. My reactions were quick, self-preserving, whereas there was always some likelihood of him freezing.

He proved as much one idle night at Bannock Street. Ian was reading and I was cross with him, probably because he was being a right bigheaded prick, pouting and tilting his chin in that way of his. I had the Webley out and was sitting on the floor yogi-style, polishing it. Then, without even planning it, I had him in my sights.

It was ages before he looked up, but I've never forgotten his face when he did. It was as if everything went out of him in a second — his breath, his blood, his wits, completely frozen.

He called me some crude things after I tossed the gun aside — a 'worthless cunt' — and said he'd put me on the moors with Pauline if I kept acting out of line. I felt rotten about it, thinking of that dark place and the beastliness of lying there forever, but there was the softest flame inside me, too. Because I had him. In that second and for all time, I had him.

I had hoped Pauline would be the only one, a moral experiment that, once executed, we would not need to repeat. Once it became clear to me that it was otherwise, however, I set my mind on making the next one better. Cleaner, more thrilling, more to his taste.

The lads were Ian's best work. John and Keith, November and June of the following year. If Ian was honest about it, he would have said it was lads he wanted all along. He was curiously timid about such things, however, and so was I. Looking back, I suppose I didn't want to think about his inclinations any more than I had to.

That they were lads, and that they were not known to me, made it easier. As sweet and lamblike as they were, the fact remained that they were lads, and Ian had been a lad too once. Also, I suppose some part of me liked it, how trustingly they got into the van with me. Because they wouldn't have, if it had been just Ian. They would have been warned against strange men.

Sitting in the van throughout, I felt less each time. I smoked, but not as much. I heard the winds, but not with any fear. I saw Ian coming back over the dark heath, after John, with the lad's left shoe in his hand. He told me how it had come off and I felt something, but quashed it quickly. We had gone too far together for me to be squeamish.

Ian was practically living at Gran's with me by that third summer, Keith's summer. There were the absences, of course, but he had started keeping many of his things there. His books, his Hitler tapes, his camera, some shirts and underwear. We had a black-and-white sheepdog together, Puppet. It was as much permanence as I could hope for, with a man like him.

We never discussed marriage, except to mock the kitchen-sink drudgery of it and everyone who went in for it. Most of my friends from school were married by that time and pregnant with their first or second babes. My younger sister Maureen was in the family way with David Smith, a petty crim and a right twit, and had to marry him before it came out. That was more of a scandal than me and Ian going quietly to our office and picnicking every weekend on the moor, where no one else ever bothered going.

We took Puppet with us, the camera, a radio, wine — always a lot of wine. In our sunglasses and sharp weekend clothes, we photographed each other among the rocks and vales. He was so handsome, so free, a king upon the heath. In my headscarves and short dresses, I was his queen.

Those detectives who've been trying to read more into our photographs, the locations of graves and so forth, have it wrong. It was always about being in our domain, and they were only a part of that, no more significant than any rock or stream.

We planned Lesley Ann for the day after Christmas, when Gran was staying in Dukinfield with my uncle. Ian spent the morning setting up the camera and lights in our bedroom. Blue photographs, he wanted. Other things, too. He didn't tell me about the tape recorder under the bed. I think he got even more of a thrill from putting one over on me.

Perhaps we both wanted a lass that time. Perhaps I wanted to prove that it wasn't just a queer thing, that it really was about challenging the order of the world, the way we talked about. Perhaps he wanted some variety. What I do know is we both saw Lesley Ann at the same time and decided on her, the way we'd once decided on each other.

A doll of a lass standing by the dodgems, looking up at the whirling fairground lights. Alone, but not unloved. We saw that even then.

She went with us gleefully and, after all the horridness, we were snowed in: Ian, myself, little Lesley Ann in her shroud of bed sheets. The snow on the roads was too thick for us to drive out to the moor, and so we sat on the settee with a bottle of Drambuie, going over things quietly. We were tender with each other that night, more tender perhaps than we'd ever been.

Of all the dreadful tests they did on me, after they first brought us in with regards to Edward's murder, one of the worst was taking a sample of my pubic hair. I was not a natural blonde, of course, but it wasn't just that; it was the invasion of what had always been between Ian and I. They were taking everything private and putting it under bright, hot lights, like a bad vaudeville play.

From the sample, they were able to determine that he and I had not been intimate for two weeks. Why that was relevant to the investigation, I don't know, but they seemed to enjoy telling me. They seemed to take any opportunity they could to undermine the tenderness that I had hunted down so determinedly.

What he has done, I have done, I told them. For months, years afterward, that was all I said. Though it wasn't the strictest truth, it was the deepest.

My sister Maureen lost the babe she had with David Smith early in the new year. I thought it a good thing and hinted that she should divorce Dave, who was too childish to make much of a husband. If she had acted on my hints, it may have ended better for all of us. Then again, what attracted Ian to Dave may always have been there, waiting to come out.

It was Ian's idea to start spending time together, the four of us; one of those ideas he got out of the clear blue that he would not elaborate on, no matter how I pressed him. In theory, I was not against keeping company with my sister of a Friday night. What got me was the way Ian had of taking Dave into a corner and conversing with him in a low voice about *our* subjects — guns, Hitler, de Sade. Meanwhile, I was relegated to empty talk of shopping and *Top of the Pops* with Maureen.

David Smith. Even now, I cannot picture him without a shudder. That greasy black mop. Those rings under his eyes, like he'd been knocked one every day of his life. Those full, slobbery lips, drinking our German wine and our Drambuie. He was seventeen, and thought a few break-ins and street fights made him hard.

'I think that lad could be a killer,' Ian said to me one night, after Dave and Maureen had crossed the street back to their house. 'With the right education.'

I told Ian to sod off and that he was daft if he thought so. He kept on it. On and on, until I reminded him of Leopold and Loeb, how things would have worked out better for them had

Loeb been a woman. Ian didn't disagree with me, didn't have to. All he had to do was smirk in that smug bastard way of his, and my logic became void.

In hindsight, there were many times when I was made to feel by Ian that my femaleness was something dull, fussy, shameful. Not intimate times, as one might expect — he was actually quite expert at overlooking it then, all the more as our fantasies progressed — but in commonplace moments, like those evenings with Dave and Maureen.

I remember once I was giving Maureen a shift dress of mine that was too tight on the hips. She tried it on and did a turn for the chaps, who both nodded then went back to their talk. In that moment, I felt what a wretched thing it was to be not only females but also females of the same stock, who shared things like dresses and uncles and beaked noses, while these unrelated men shared whiskey and intimacies we could never know.

Another occasion, I remember the chaps going out to take a piss in the alley while we remained inside. It was a miserable night, bucketing down, and when they came back in they were soaked through. 'Why didn't you just use the loo upstairs like normal people?' Maureen asked them. They just giggled together, the bastards, and I knew immediately that the adventure of it was preferable to any warm, well-lit corner we could offer.

I wasn't involved in any of the planning for Edward. Partly because Ian didn't care to involve me, partly because there was no plan. My clever clerk had decided to wing it, for the fresh thrill of it.

I was there when he brought the lad home, though, under no duress: a gangly, limp-wristed lad the same age as David Smith. I hung back as Ian poured him wine and entertained him on the settee and, when he called for me to fetch Dave from across the street, I did. Furious as I was, there was something in me that burned to see Dave's face turn green, to hand Ian the proof that I was far more capable than any slobbery-lipped git he might choose to piss down alleys with.

'Ian has some miniature wines for you,' I told Dave when he opened his front door, and even the sight of Maureen yawning in her housecoat, hair a black bird's nest, did nothing for me.

It was the messiest yet. Fourteen axe blows about the head and neck, though we didn't learn the exact number until later. It is difficult for most people to imagine that kind of carnage, the almost surreal excess of it — blood on the curtains, tufts of hair in the fireplace, shards of bone scattered across the floor like beads. In the middle of it all stood Ian, shirt bespattered and a dark strand hanging over his forehead, but otherwise clean.

We worked until four in the morning, getting rid of all traces of forensic. We did a fair job. If anybody skimped, it was Dave. He sat with us afterward in the curtained sitting room, sipping tea. His hands shook. Ours didn't. Ian should have done him in then. He was a right twit, trusting David Smith.

Perhaps it was wrong of me to love a tender man. Tender is so close to weak, and weak cannot be trusted. Weak is useless in a crisis.

We had talked about what we would do if it came to it, going out in a blaze of gunfire then turning our weapons on each other.

We would be brave and honourable like the Nazis in the bunker. It did not happen that way.

I remember so clearly, how I came downstairs to see Ian sat on the settee. He was wearing only underwear and writing himself a sick note. He had sat up all night and was too tired to go into the office, he said. I looked at him, huddled with his biro and his writing pad, and wanted to hold him to my breast and nurse him, he seemed so tender. Then came the knock at the door and everything went out of him, the tenderness included.

Some nights, when the pipes are clanging and the darkness too solid for me to see my own hand through, that old fear returns. I feel black things gathering above me, the fragility of roofs and walls. I am alone.

My hair is back to its natural colour, dark as peat soil. I am heavy and dull, yet places within me remain soft. I like to go to the chapel and look at the waxy Christ faces, smell the incense on the air. I like to feel the organ notes tugging within me, stronger than any fear or desire. I like to think that we are all still children on this darkened earth.

Charlie's Girls

We all leave home looking for something that isn't there. Family, you could call it. Togetherness. Or maybe just plain Love. Whatever it is, it's not waiting for us inside those little lighted boxes on their little green hillsides with their little flags waving in front. It's not at our kitchen tables or on the laps of our daddies. And you better believe it's not on our TV screens.

Some of us come from afar, nasal New England toy towns and Rust Belt backwoods. Most of us come from closer. Santa Marina. San Gabriel. Redondo. You've probably seen us walking in the sunshine, tanned all year round, with our books pressed to our chests. We're dreamy and don't like chemistry or violin lessons. When we talk, it's in dull, sultry tones; the heat that cracks the asphalt.

Some of us are cheerleaders, choirgirls, homecoming queens. Some of us are wallflowers, just learning to let our hair down. We are all, without exception, beautiful — inside and out. Christ made us that way, but not the Christ *you* believe in.

Our daddies are veterans. They have cruel, boring jobs like 'headmaster' and 'stockbroker' and 'aeronautical engineer'. Our mothers are dead or homemakers. They care about Glo-Coat and cry every day of the week. There's no Love there.

It's in Haight-Ashbury for a while, for those of us who get there early enough. After that, we have to look for it in wilder places, in the canyons and campervans beside the road. But none of us find it for real until Charlie.

Because if Love has a human form, it's him. A man of thirty-three with a cleft in his chin and all the darkness of locked prison cells in his eyes. He talks quietly, but everyone listens. He isn't tall and strong like some G.I. Joe, but he doesn't need to be. When he looks at us, it's pure awareness, light coming to the surface and mingling with the dark, of which it is born and the same.

And he knows us, body and soul.

It's all Love. Life or death, birthing or killing, it doesn't matter. We killed them because we love them and now we're standing in the living room, tripping over how good it looks. Rope hanging from the rafters. Bloody writing on the walls. Stuff scattered everywhere. Candleholders, ashtrays, matchbooks, potted plants. On the sofa, a big fat American flag.

People think death is ugly, but if you look at it with pure awareness, it's the most beautiful thing in the world. Like all the sound and all the colour and all the beauty all at once. But the colours are fading on us and time is creeping back, oozy and slow to start with, then itching. We always listen to the animals inside our bodies, the writhing snakes and jumping rabbits and crawling insects. And they're all telling us one thing — *vámonos*.

Out of that lit-up glasshouse, we run barefoot and night blooms around us, fragrant with hedges and bodies and blowing pine trees. The car is waiting at the bottom of the hill and Darling is clutching the wheel. Tex tells her to get over and she does and we all pile in, shivering in our wet creepy-crawlies. It's wild how the blood chilled on us when it was so warm and groovy before. Kinda like cum, dribbling hot one second and Jell-O cold the next.

We get naked as Tex winds the car around and around, past leafy clumps and freaky-tall palm trees and splashes of papery red flowers. There's angry streaks all over our skin, running down our thighs and bellies. Sadie touches her red fingers to her cunt and says, 'Aunt Flo is in town!' which gets us all giggling. Then we get talking about what went down at the house.

'That bitch pulled my hair,' says Katie, who's got the most magical brown hair, lush and long to her waist. 'I got a killer headache.'

Sadie tries to one-up her by telling how the big dude beaned her, but Katie won't be beat. 'Man, my bones hurt. I kept stabbin' and hittin' bones and now my bones hurt.' That makes Tex laugh his big, hawing donkey laugh.

'Y'all heard their bones crack when I kicked 'em? *Kkkk-chhhh!*'

Darling is the only one of us without a story to tell, since she was on lookout the whole time. Tex wants her to get her hands dirty too, so he tells her to hop out at this big ravine. Then he peels off his creepy-crawlies and passes them through the window, motioning us to do the same. Darling looks freaked over how wet the clothes are, and even more when Tex hands her the gun and knives. 'No one's goin' to see these for a million years. Get it?'

We all watch Darling walk in the moonlight to the edge of the ravine. The backseat's leather feels cool against our backs, sexy. She throws everything down, drippy with blood, then squints into the darkness. Back in the car, she shows us her red hands.

The next afternoon, in the back ranch, we're all glued to the TV set like little kids watching *Looney Tunes*. They keep showing pictures of the people from the house, especially the blonde, who was an actress and about to drop a baby. '... She was all like "My baby, my baby!" and I said, "Look bitch, I don't care about you or your baby. You're gonna die, so you better be ready."' Sadie takes a toke and passes it along. The TV picture changes from the actress to the brunette, some kinda coffee heiress. 'That's the bitch that pulled my hair!' says Katie. We all boo and hiss, since Katie's hair is magical; Charlie says we're all gonna use it as a blanket someday when we go into the desert.

A little while later, Charlie wanders in and we all go quiet. Or maybe it's a long while later and we're already quiet, sprawling on the trailer floor. Either way, there's Charlie's voice and we all hear it, faraway like we're underwater, but knife-clear. He says, 'You done good.' We see his beautiful feet, his legs in tight buckskin. 'Same deal tonight, but one more chick. Who's it gonna be?'

That's enough to get all of us sitting up, waving our hands and chiming, 'Pick me, pick me, Charlie!' But out of everyone, he decides on LuLu. She's Bobby's girl and has only fucked Charlie two or three times, so we're not sure why he chooses her. 'Are you crazy enough to believe in me?' he asks LuLu, fixing her with his gun barrel stare. She stares back at him with her long-lashed beauty queen eyes. When she gets his signal, she yips like a coyote.

It's late and most of us are sitting around the bonfire when the group takes off. We don't really notice them going, except in a far-off way, but we see them getting back at daybreak, waving at some dude in a Chevy they hitched with. They look fresh and happy in their change of clothes, telling stories about how easy it was. LuLu says they even hung around for a couple of hours after, taking showers and chugging chocolate milk from the fridge.

'We played with their dogs, too,' she says. 'Little fluffy white balls!'

A couple of days later, the ranch gets raided. Most of us are sleeping when the pigs storm in, kicking down doors and pointing M-15s. They drag us up by our hair and haul us out to the driveway, making us kneel in the dust with the guns aimed at our heads. Charlie always says the bigger the gun, the smaller the dick, and you can tell that's how it is with these dudes. They've got bellies and buzz-cuts and dinky helmets, and the word 'Sheriff' sewn onto the backs of their uniforms. There's even a couple of copters flying overhead, like it's fucking Nam or something.

'Where's your guru now?' the pigs smirk. 'Looks like Jesus is savin' his own skin.' We cuss them out, telling them Charlie doesn't have to show his face if he doesn't want to, that he can take any form he wants — a bird in the sky, wind through the trees, even a bit of dust on their nasty black boots. But eventually, a couple of them come out from around the barn with Charlie in cuffs. 'Found this chicken-shit hiding under the porch.'

Charlie gives us a sign with his eyes and we all go off, howling and yipping and calling out, 'Right on, Charlie!' It's a long time before they can shut us up and read out what we're charged with: *grand theft auto*. We start yipping again as soon as we hear that.

'Crazy bitches,' is all those pigs can say.

We're out of the slam within two weeks on insufficient evidence. The ranch looks like it's been hit by a tornado, windows smashed in and cars confiscated and tumbleweed blowing across the drive. Darling and a couple of the newer chicks have split, probably back to their folks to get fat and become good little secretaries. Charlie takes us into the old saloon to look at the mural we painted a few months back. It shows the end of time, all in Day-Glo colours; the desert and valleys and Helter Skelter coming from the sky. 'It's now,' Charlie tells us. 'It's comin' down fast.'

Death Valley is full of life if you know where to look. We find the skulls of bighorn sheep buried in the sand, antlers turned to rust. Chuckwallas scrambling into sagebrush. All kinds of groovy, night-blooming plants — spiked white cereus, sacred datura, moonlight cactus. Black skies swirling with stars and big, dusty moons. All night, coyotes howl from the outcrops.

Then there are the spiders, the scorpions, the rattlers. We lie down on the burning rocks and commune with them, watch their beautiful spines in motion and stare into their shiny black eyes. There's no fear there, just wisdom; the kind that comes from millions of years of killing. They stare back without blinking.

Slowly, they run their coils over our skin.

'See the snake?' Charlie's face flickers in the campfire. 'See him on his belly? That's the Devil, man. That's J.C. He's tuned in. He lives a hundred years a second, dig?'

Here in the desert, with our knives strapped to our ankles, it doesn't take much to turn animal. If Charlie says snake, we become the snake. If he says coyote, we become the coyote. If he says stab, it's moonlight and bleeding silver, baby. We dance in circles around the fire, slashing at whatever gets in our way. One time, Charlie gives us a sign to slash him, so we do, tearing at his body till all that's left is a warm, loving ooze. Then we turn around and see him standing naked under the moon, fully resurrected, wearing a crown of creosote. Man, it's a trip.

Jesus is always fucking with people's heads. They never taught us that in Sunday school, but it's the truth. Water into wine. Death into life. Nothing into everything. That's Love. That's Christ. That's Charlie.

The dudes drive into camp with stolen cars, strip them down, and use the parts to build dune buggies. Someday, we're gonna have hundreds of dune buggies, hidden all over the desert. We're gonna mount machine guns on top of them so the guys can shoot while we drive, then we're gonna swoop down on all the little towns and kill anyone who isn't beautiful.

But the pigs have eyes on us, even out here. One night, coming back from the hot springs, we almost drive right into this trap they set for us — a big fat hole in the middle of the trail. Next to it is a big fat pile of dirt and a bigger, fatter yellow digging truck.

'Who-zam!' Charlie points and hollers when he sees it. Then we all hop out of the dune buggy.

As Charlie deals with the truck, we start filling the hole. 'You come into my desert with your beast machines, you set your rabbit traps, you light your fires ...' He lets out the fuel, pours some gas. Before he's even done it, we see the flames jumping out of his fingertips.

The pigs don't quit there. They fly their planes low over the desert, trying to flush us out, but we're snaky. We keep low with our knives, staying under rocks and tarpaulins. One meal a day is enough for us. One little cup of water. One word in our heads: Love.

After dark, we go to work fortifying our camp, digging hide-outs and rigging up barbed-wire traps. Charlie has this far-out idea of building a wall of human skulls and tells us how to boil the flesh from the bones. When we ask whose skulls we should use, he says, 'Pigs, Judases, bitches. Heck, use Kitty here. She got a pretty head.'

Kitty is Charlie's favourite punching bag lately, since she's always playing the weak link, trying to get special treatment for being knocked up. We end up wishing we did take her head a few nights later, when we find she's skedaddled with this other preg-nant chick, Steph. We run out with our knives drawn, ready to christen the dark, but the trail goes cold. Turns out those sneaky pigs got to them first.

Everyone wants us to be afraid of death. If we're not afraid, that means we don't feel guilty, and if we're not guilty, that means death isn't the ugly thing they think it is. They want to keep death in the dark so bad, they can't see that it's everywhere beauty is — laughing in the street, throwing flowers, making love in long grass, dancing to beautiful music that comes in waves of red and green and purple.

Charlie says Jesus died with a hard-on and a sweet, sexy smile on his face. He knows because he lived it 2,000 years ago. He'll live it again, if he has to. Already, he's X-ed himself out of this world. We all have. That's what the X we burned onto our foreheads stands for: we're done, we're giving up the system.

That bitch Darling turned state's evidence. We all send black vibes her way while she's sitting on the witness stand, talking about how horrible it was to hear those people screaming. It's wacked how she can sit there, looking prissy and crying her eyes out, when she's been touched by Charlie. It's all gonna come back to get her, just you wait. Karma has special punishments in store for Judases like that.

Sitting around in court every day is a drag, especially when they're always sending Charlie out for speaking truth. Our attorneys bring us drawing pads and coloured pencils, so we can pass some of the time doodling skulls and kittens and whatever. It kinda feels like being back in kindergarten, but it sure beats listening to those old dudes running their mouths all day.

Even though the trial's been going on a few months, the TV people keep hanging around outside the courtroom, waiting to get a shot of the three of us in our hand-sewn outfits, made special by the girls outside — velveteen pantsuits for Katie, see-through blouses for Sadie, flouncy dresses for LuLu. We're

Charlie's girls. Our hands are linked and our hair flows long and lush. We smile big for the cameras and raise our voices in song.

Always is always forever
Is one is one is one
Inside yourself for your father
All is one all is one all is none

We sing for all those girls outside, who we love. For our daddies hiding behind their newspapers, our mommies crying over burnt meatloaf. For all the square-eyed people watching us on television. Until the whole world knows we're not afraid, we'll keep singing.

Jan

Cam gives me the box on the night of our three-month anniversary, parked out in the woods in his red pickup. It's a small box made of cedar, just the size to keep jewellery or photographs. Two brass hinges on the inside and a frilly brass lock on the outside. So polished the moon dances in its red wood.

'See how dark it is, honey?' Cam runs his huge hands along it and there's no more moon, just shadows. 'That's the best stuff. Heartwood. I saw it at work and thought of you.'

Cam works at the lumber mill. So do his dad and his brother Dex. All three of them tall men, shy of their height, with shaggy blond hair and small features bunched in the middle of their faces. I like to look at Cam's dad sometimes and pretend I'm looking at Cam in twenty years.

'Oh, Cam.' I look down. Already my glasses are fogging. 'I don't deserve it.'

His lips curl upward and then they're pushing against mine, giving me a sick, fizzy feeling deep in my stomach. Three months and I still don't know what Cam's doing with me, how he can stand looking at my pudgy nose and frizzy hair and the rosy acne on my cheeks, let alone kissing me.

After a while, Cam puts his hand under my blouse and leaves it there. I can hear a creek trickling in the dark and a nightjar churring somewhere in the bushes. My heart beating in the middle of these woods, louder than anything.

Cam's favourite movies are scary and his favourite holiday is Halloween. He says he likes the costumes, the hoods and masks especially, and the way everyone gets to spend the night being someone else. I can't help wondering if he'd still like these things so much if he knew about the secrets I'm hiding.

The first time it happened, I thought it was beautiful. There was this shimmering on the air and a ringing in my ears like church bells, only just for me. Mom and Lisa were peeling potatoes at the counter with me, but it was like I was looking down on them from heaven. The next thing I knew, I was on the floor with a taste of blood in my mouth and my whole family standing around me.

Their eyes said it all: *Jan's got the Devil in her.*

I never know when the Devil is going to show up: if I'll be at my school desk or watching cartoons in the den or picking apples out back in the orchard. But he never shows when I'm with Cam, not even on Halloween or the night we go to see *The Exorcist*. Watching that demon girl shaking on screen, I wait for the worst. Then Cam gives me his hand.

One Wednesday after school, I go downtown with Mom and Lisa to get my eyes tested. Mrs Kimble said I probably need a new prescription, since I'm having trouble seeing the board. I guess she's right, but my eyes still work well enough to see the look Mom gives Lisa when the doctor reads my results.

I've been secretly wishing for a new pair of glasses, maybe some with pink frames or coloured lenses. But Mom just tells them to set the thick new lenses in my old wire frames, and I walk out looking uglier than ever.

'Well, I hope you're grateful, Jan,' Mom gripes. 'I paid through the nose for those lenses.'

'She'll have to bring home Bs from now on!' Lisa says.

Mom and Lisa think this is a riot, I guess because even in their wildest dreams, I'm only a B student. Not like Lisa, who's so good at everything my parents wanted her to go the secretary school instead of marrying Bobby Norton. Now her and Bobby have a little house of their own on Pine Street, and Lisa is expecting.

I walk behind them toward Lisa's car, parked across from the post office. Her legs turn out in a funny way and the veins look pretty, bright-green against her white skin. I'm concentrating so hard on Lisa's veins I don't see anything else and almost bump into her when she halts in front of me.

'Is that Cameron?' She points across the street. 'Coming out of the post office?'

I crane my neck. Sure enough, there he is, walking out with a brown-paper package and a solemn look on his face. He glances around, but he doesn't seem to see us. Then he slips the package under his jacket and puts his head down, like he's going out in a storm without an umbrella.

'Such a serious young man,' my mom says.

I don't know why, but the air starts shimmering then.

Cam doesn't say anything about my glasses when we next meet, and I don't say anything about seeing him downtown. He buys me a root beer and drives us to a part of the woods where the sun's already set. I feel my stomach fizzing as we pull off the dirt track.

'Cam?' My voice is a stupid squeak. 'Cam, I need to tell you something …'

And just like that, it all spills out of me: about the fits, about the church bells in my ears, about the looks my family give me and all the money I'm costing them. I tell him that he shouldn't be with me, that there's too much wrong with me. He's quiet through all of it, one big hand still on the wheel. I hiccup and my glasses fall off my face, right onto the floor of the pickup.

'Oh, Cam! Oh, I'm sorry!'

It's so dark, and my eyes so blurry, I have to dig between my knees to find them. Still Cam doesn't say anything. Scary pictures flash through my head: Cam booting me out of the truck, Cam driving off, Cam leaving me alone in the woods all night. Then I feel his big hands reaching through the dark, wiping my tears.

'Shhh, honey. Shhh. Come here.'

In his arms, my body judders like a chainsaw. He keeps shushing me as I breathe in salty gulps. After a while, all that's left for him to shush are wet sounds. I swallow a lump of spit. I sniff against his shirtfront. His plaid smells like woodchips and something sweet, maybe resin or cologne.

'I'll make you better,' Cam says. 'I'll make it all better.'

Lisa's baby has just started kicking. She shows me one evening when I'm over at her house, getting help with my homework while she does macramé. Doing macramé is just about Lisa's favourite thing now that she's pregnant. She's made macramé clothes for the baby, and macramé blankets, and even a macramé cradle swing. I want her to teach me, but she says I have to do my math homework first. Knowing me, I'd probably mess it up anyway.

I'm trying to figure out a problem, something about a farmer with ten Thanksgiving turkeys, when Lisa makes a funny sound behind me. 'Ouf!' She grabs her belly. 'Someone just woke up in a bad mood!'

'Who?'

She stares at me like I'm stupid and keeps rubbing her belly until I realise she means the baby. I put down my homework and scooch up to the sofa. It's quiet for a while. Then Lisa laughs softly and puts my hands on the swelling under her paisley dress.

'Feel him?' she asks.

There's a rippling beneath my palms, like water in a creek.

'Yeah. I think so.'

Across the room, the clock chimes seven. Lisa smiles and picks up her macramé again, tells me Bobby will be home any minute. I think of Cam when she says that, how he'd look coming through the door of a house just like this one, and it's a nice thought.

Something funny happens to Cam about the third time we make love. Not ha-ha funny, but the other kind, where my face gets hot and the back of my eyes start stinging. He rubs himself, but nothing happens. He cusses. He draws his big, long body away from mine.

'I'm sorry, Cam ...' I start.

I don't know why but that makes him cuss again. Then he looks down at my stupid fat chest and laughs, a mean sound like a bark. I cover myself and he sits up, picks my glasses up from the dashboard. For a minute, I think he's going to do something cruel like snap them or toss them out the window. But he doesn't.

'Are you really sorry, Jan?' Cam says, his voice like clouds scudding over the moon.

'Yes, of course!'

'Maybe you can do something for me then.'

'Anything.'

'Close your eyes.'

I do what he says, even though it gives me goosebumps. He clicks open the glove compartment and takes something out of it, dumps it in my lap. Then he fixes my glasses over my eyes.

'Open up, honey.'

There's a magazine open to a picture of a naked lady tied up with something around her mouth. Her eyes look big, and her private parts are all on show like a skinned rabbit. Cam turns the page and there's another lady tied up, this time on her knees with her rear-end facing the camera. Next, a lady hanging with her arms over her head and her hair falling over her face. She looks different from the others, a bit like those pictures of Jesus being killed.

'I think you'd look real pretty like this.' Cam points at the hanging lady. 'What do you think?'

There are bits of snow by the road so small they look like lumps of trash. I see them flashing in the dark as Cam drives us deeper. I don't know what he's looking for or how he knows when he's found it, but it gives me the creeps nonetheless.

'We'll walk from here,' he says, after he's parked and pulled his keys from the ignition. 'You can get out, honey.'

I open the door. The ground feels soft under my sneakers, somewhere between fall-leaf crunch and winter squelch. Cam stays in the truck for a minute. When he comes out, he's got some kind of toolbox with him and a camera around his neck. He tells me to walk ahead.

'But I don't know where we're going, Cam.'

'You let me worry about that. You just stay in front now.'

I never knew I could be so embarrassed about the way my hips move or how my rear-end looks in jeans. I tug down my sweater and duck my head, fighting the urge to look back at Cam every step I take. It hurts, not being allowed to do what's most normal to me.

'Stop here,' Cam says after a while. There's a tall tree in front of us, maybe a cedar. Then he says, 'Take your clothes off.'

Even though he's seen me undressed before, it's different out here. I shiver and look around, thinking maybe he'll change his mind if he sees how cold and lonely it is. But he just puts down his toolbox and starts sorting through it. I squat on the wet ground and tug at my shoelaces, trying to remember the rhyme Lisa taught me when I was little. *Bunny ears, bunny ears, playing by a tree. Crisscross the tree, trying to catch me ...*

'Cam? My socks are all wet.'

'Shhh.' He keeps going through the box. I hear metal, glimpse something shiny. 'A little water never hurt anyone, did it?'

I don't tell him my jeans are wet too, or my sweater, or my bra and panties when I'm down to them. A soft rain fogs the air between us. Cam closes the box and comes toward me, his hands full of hooks and chains.

'Your underwear, too,' he tells me. 'And your glasses.'

The cold from the woods stays with me, even after Cam hauls me down and unchains me and makes love to me. Even after he lets me put my clothes back on and gives me his jacket for the hike back to the truck. Even in his pickup, when he gets me to put my hands in front of the heater because they look so blue. 'We've just gotta get the blood running again,' he tells me, blowing on them and rubbing them between his. Then, sorry-sounding, 'Next time, I won't leave you up so long.'

The Devil comes to me the morning after, when I'm sick in bed with the flu. I can't stop him getting inside or even call out, my breath flies out of me so fast. Then I'm on the floor with my bedclothes hanging over me, looking up at Cam's heartwood box on my nightstand. It looks so huge in that moment I swear I could fit right inside it.

It snows the week before Christmas, and Cam asks my parents' permission to take me skiing. They say yes, since he's big and strong and sensible, and since his brother Dex is coming, too. I sit between them on the drive up to Lassen Peak, and they spook me by talking about how it's actually a volcano. I ask if it can explode with us up there.

'Sure, honey.' Cam smiles. 'Blow us all to smithereens.'

'Even with snow on it?'

'Uh-huh. We'll just be real cold before it burns us up.'

But when we get there, both the boys are sweet to me. Cam fixes a knitted cap on my head and says I make a real cute snow bunny. Then they help me put my skis on and show me how to keep them straight, how to slow down by making a V-shape. Even though Cam and Dex have been skiing their whole lives, they're happy to stay on the little slopes with me until I've had enough. After that, Dex walks me down to the lodge and says something that makes me blush. 'My brother talks about you all the time, you know.'

The sky is dark blue by the time we load everything back into Cam's pickup. Dex takes the wheel so I can rest my head on Cam's shoulder and listen without listening as they talk about the slopes and the guys at the mill. After a million winding mountain passes, the road gets straight and the woods beside it thicker. Then the woods turn into orchards and paddocks, trailer parks and motels, the lit-up Jolly Kone sign.

'Pull over here,' Cam says. He nudges my head from his shoulder. 'Hungry, Jan?'

I nod sleepily. Dex pulls into the parking lot and Cam starts giving him our orders, like it's already decided that the two of us will stay in the truck. I watch Dex slam the door and slump across to the restaurant. I like Dex, who's closer to my age than Cam and maybe even more handsome, but that doesn't explain why I'm so sorry to see him go.

'I've been meaning to show you something,' Cam turns to me.

A minute later, he's reaching into the glove box, and I can't help thinking of the dirty magazines he keeps there. Then I see it's not a magazine but photographs. All out of focus, too dark in places and too bright in others.

'They're a bit blurry, but your poses turned out real nice. See?'

He points to a white smudge in the middle of one shot and things start taking shape — branches and fuzzy rain and my dark hair hanging in my face.

My face gets hotter as Cam keeps going through the pictures, using bad words to talk about parts of my body. I've never heard him use words like that, but he says them as calmly as he'd say anything else. He's just as calm a few minutes later, hiding the photos in his jacket when Dex bangs on the truck's roof. I jump, just like if we were caught necking.

'Cheeseburger, double burger.' Dex hands us our food and grins. 'Hope I'm not, uh, interrupting.'

The more pregnant Lisa gets, the more I wish I could ask her about how she got that way. But the one time I bring up her and

Bobby, whether they did more than neck before they were married, her face goes mean. 'That's personal, Jan.' A little while later, she says, 'Nice guys don't marry fast girls.'

Cam hangs me up in the woods again. I tell him every time that I don't like it, but he sounds so sure of his rightness, telling me all the effort he went to making some special cuffs and how pretty he finds me, and how it's good for a woman to feel pain, that's how God made us. And even though it's scarier than the Devil, Cam is always real nice to me afterward, kissing me and cuddling me and wrapping me in a big wool blanket so I don't catch cold again.

Mostly Cam takes photographs when I'm up there. Sometimes he puts a blindfold on me and does other things. One time, he blindfolds my mouth and says he's going to use a cat-o-nine-tails on me. I don't know what he means, but when he gets it out of his toolbox, I start crying.

For my sixteenth birthday, my parents let me have Cam over for dinner. He wears a blazer jacket that's too short at the cuffs, and combs his shaggy hair to one side. I blow-dry my hair and wear an old dress of Lisa's, let out at the bust to fit me. Mom cooks my favourite chicken with lemon and herbs. For dessert, there's chocolate Bundt cake.

My family are nicer to me with Cam there, and Cam is nice, too. It's like they're all trying to make a good impression, with me in the middle of it all, not being told I've got the Devil in me or to do my homework for once. After I blow out all my candles, Cam takes a small wrapped box from the pocket of his blazer, and for a second I think maybe he's going to kneel. But he stays where he is and watches me pull the ribbon, and instead it's a thin silver chain with a heart-shaped pendant.

'Oh, Cam, it's *pretty*,' I whisper and touch the pendant.

With my parents' permission, he puts it on for me, his big hands fumbling over the tiny links. It fits right against my throat, almost like a collar, but so light I can barely feel it. All the rest of the night, I keep reaching up to touch it, just to make sure it's still there.

The baby comes in April, around the same time as the blossoms on our apple trees. Lisa names him Bobby Jr and brings him over to see us, wrapped in a bright macramé blanket. I'm supposed to be studying, but I'm allowed to take some time out to meet Bobby Jr. I'm even allowed to hold him for a minute, his red face all closed up like a rosebud, before Lisa gets worried I'll have a fit and drop him.

Cam picks me up from school one afternoon, just after my last math test of the year. He doesn't usually get off work until four o'clock, but there was an accident at the mill, so everyone got sent home early. 'Gil lost a thumb in the chipper,' he tells me with a big smile. 'There was blood spurting everywhere, you should've seen it.' Then he says he'll buy me a root beer.

It's sunny so we stand out in the Jolly Kone parking lot, leaning and squinting against the pickup. I tell Cam I think I failed my test, and he says that's okay, girls don't need to be good at math. Then I start telling him about Bobby Jr, how much bigger he's getting, the lace he'll be wearing for his christening. I guess

Cam is sick of hearing about Bobby Jr, since he stops me there. He picks up my hand.

'You know, Jan, we've been dating almost a year now.'

'Uh-huh. One year on June thirty.'

'That's right, honey. And, you know, I'm really grateful for all the things you do for me, even though they may be a little, uh, uncomfortable.'

'Uh-huh,' I say, more quietly this time.

'Well, there's something I've been meaning to ask you …'

Cam starts describing it, slowly and calmly. It sounds so crazy I think I must be hearing him wrong. Not scary, like the hanging. Just plain crazy.

'A creek, Cam …?' I ask, and can't help but scrunch up my nose.

A wind blows across the parking lot, shaking the restaurant's awning, bringing sweet smells from the orchards around town. Apple blossoms. Plum blossoms. Walnuts and almonds. Cam smiles, squeezes my hand.

'Think how pretty you'll look in the water, honey. Like a mermaid.'

As soon as we get out of the truck, I hear the water trickling. Other sounds, too, rustling and ribbiting and the rumbling of night birds and insects. Everything in the woods has a sound for what I'm feeling. When I take off my clothes at the bank, mosquitoes fly to the back of my knees and ankles.

Cam takes off some clothes, too: his boots and his trousers. It's not much, but it leaves him more naked than usual, so he seems almost shy telling me, 'Put your hands behind your back.' I do what he says, ducking my head while he cuffs me. It reminds me of the time he did up my necklace. All of a sudden, I wish I could touch the pendant, but it's too late. He's holding me by the elbows.

'Go on,' Cam says.

Water swishes around my ankles, then his ankles, then my knees. As soon as it gets above them, he tells me to kneel, like a baptism. The water bubbles up into my privates, cold and dirty. I yelp, and I guess that does something to Cam's mood. He knees me in the back, so hard it's a shock to me. Then he grabs hold of my hair.

'*Breathe*,' he says, like it's a dirty word.

But I can't breathe when the water hits. There's only tiny bubbles, a darkness around my head that gets thicker. He pulls me up just long enough for me to feel the wetness, before dragging me under again. This time, there's a clunking in my ears, a sour taste in my mouth, things scraping and bursting inside me.

It keeps happening, up and down, like a shaking I can't stop. Then I'm on the bank and can't hear or feel anything, though I can see Cam gritting his teeth above me. Kicking. His face so mean I know it's not him trampling my ribs, but the Devil. I close my eyes. I open them. Sounds rush back into the world.

'Shhh, honey. Shhh.' Cam is crouching next to me, smiling. 'I'm here.'

I ask Cam to come and see me after Bobby Jr's christening, in the apple orchard behind my house. The blossoms have fruited into tiny green apples, not ripe enough to eat yet. I play with one of the apples while I wait for him, rolling it between my hands. It keeps me from picking at the mosquito bites, all scabbed along my arms and legs.

I hear Cam's pickup door slamming out front. He comes around the side of the house, still wearing his shirt and tie, but no jacket. He's got a big smile that gets smaller as he gets closer. His eyebrows go up.

'You wanted to talk, honey?'

I nod but don't say anything. I give him the apple then take it back. My glasses start fogging. Cam hugs me. He loves me, I think.

'We're having a baby,' I tell him, my voice just a whisper. He doesn't say anything, just keeps hugging me.

People are nicer to me now that they think I'm having a baby. For one thing, I don't have to go to school anymore, which means no more homework and no exams. For another thing, Lisa is teaching me how to macramé — blankets for the baby, and holders for our kitchen herbs, and a kind of over-the-shoulder bag, which she says will come in real handy for carrying baby things.

For another, the Devil hasn't bothered me once since our wedding night in Reno.

My parents wanted us married quick and cheap, so they sent us across the state line to do it, just me and Cam and $500 in cash. We went to one of those chapels with the neon lights and paper hearts over the altar, and afterward they gave us a free chicken dinner and a little cake in the shape of church bells.

I've been eating well and hope it's only a matter of time before I'm pregnant for real. I feel bad about lying, and Cam has been so nice and loving lately. Every day, he goes to work at the mill and doesn't complain, and most weeks he brings home free lumber for his projects. There's a basement here, so he can work on them whenever he wants without disturbance.

Cam doesn't like being disturbed in the basement, which suits me just fine. I don't much like going down there either, on account of it being where he keeps his toolbox and camera and all those other things. So long as I don't see those things, it's mostly easy to forget them, like they're all hidden away in a box I don't have any key for. But sometimes, even without looking, something ordinary will remind me — running water or hanging laundry or even just the shade of a tree — and I'll feel my heart start beating like we're in the middle of the woods again.

Marceline

Our crops fail, but our babies grow strong and sweet, like the sweetest pea-snaps. Every colour imaginable, every mix of every colour. God never intended to keep the races separate. Such prejudice could only come from the hearts of men, their infinite fear and folly. Sometimes, wandering through the nursery, I think of those stories of babies found in bulrushes, cabbage patches, and it's a nice thought: that babies might truly crop up that way, from the pureness of the earth, free from the frailties of men.

Thirty-three born right here in Jonestown. Did you ever see such healthy, happy babies? And not one of them who ever has to experience America's racism.

Our cribs are reinforced with mesh to keep out creepy-crawlies. Our wall hangings and hand-braided rugs are made of red, green, yellow, black: the colours of our adoptive nation. On the verandah, picture books bloom in the laps of our women, who nurture our babies' minds with daily storytime. Many of our three-year-olds already know their ABCs. Of course this's the first they ever heard of NBC.

Some of you men laugh. A tight, showy kinda laugh, but at a time like this that's to be expected.

We didn't want media. We didn't want congressmen. We wanted to be left in peace. That you all couldn't give us that much is proof of the enormity of what we've done: a thousand men, women, and children turning our backs on the United States for a simpler life down here in the jungle. But we're making the best of this intrusion. Last night when the congressman came onstage to praise our community, the applause was so loud it almost brought down the roof of the pavilion.

We are nothing if not a proud people, an optimistic people.

Here we have the kitchen, where Sister Liliana and her crew prepare three thousand nutritious meals each day. The woodshop, where Brother Ernie and his crew construct everything from bunk beds to pull-along toys. The piggery; see how good and fat our sows are, our beauteous Blissie who is mother to eighteen piglets. Each plank we walk along was measured, sawed, and laid by our construction crew. Each person treading these paths is brother or sister to the next. Such close-knit community you'd be lucky to find nowadays even in the smallest Midwestern town, where people no longer feel safe leaving their doors unlocked.

There is no crime here in Jonestown, no dispute that can't be resolved communally.

That knot of people by the pavilion, drawing more in like a tornado; I wouldn't pay it any mind. There are less of you than when this tour began. Stay behind me, please; don't stray. I know the sun is hot, and these flies are a nuisance, but we have many more sights to see, people to meet, refreshments awaiting us at the end of the line.

A pair of sisters whisk by. Another sister, our Esme who works so hard in the laundry, whispers in my ear, and what she says — well, that's not for you to know. Maybe you few who haven't yet snuck away notice my face tense; you newsmen are trained to notice every frown, tic, averted eye. But when I next speak, it's with a smile.

A good first lady, in the face of crisis, always finds some way to smile.

In the pavilion's shade, the afternoon looks hourless. I see my husband's face from afar, the broad slack lines of it, and want nothing more than to lay him down and cover him with a cool sheet, tell him to sleep away this defeat. *Sleep, Jim, just sleep.* It's true what Sister Esme said; there's folks deserting, and the who and how many of it doesn't matter because it's plain he's taking it personally. Always, in the more than thirty years I've known him, he's been the kind to take things personal: the sufferings of others, their individual pains, but most of all their betrayals.

You can't keep them all, Jim, I've tried telling him. You can't hold them like cards to your chest.

The Morrises, one of our oldest white families. With us since Indiana, those ugly pre-integration days when just the claim 'all men are equal' could have folks burning crosses on our lawns, painting swastikas on our church stairs. So many hard times lived through together: Sister Judy, surely you recall how you came to us weeping after the drowning of your little boy in '59? Brother Gerald, the years of alcoholism and the friends who got you through it, friends who are still here today? Will you truly leave behind all us here who love you? Will you truly turn your back on this life we've made?

It isn't what we expected, Sister Judy says grimly. It isn't what we were told.

Her eyes holding mine, glassy blue-green like mine, the skin around them cracked with wrinkles like mine. After a certain age, women like us — women who've worked hard and suffered much — we all start looking the same.

Brother Gerald can barely look at me, but when he does, his eyes are the sad brown of a dog with a broken leg. Then he lets them drop in my husband's direction, and without planning on it, I'm seeing what they see: Jim, a dry-lipped ghost, hiding behind his dark glasses. He's trying to squeeze little Billy Barnhart's shoulder, frowning into his pimento-red shirt when Billy flinches. Nearby, his California college girls huddle with our lawyers, their slim legs crossed, lips working quick and snide. The big, bearish congressman whispers with his aide. Our security detail keep watch over the media, arms folded and faces gloomy as the gathering clouds.

There's no words for it. No happy words, anyways.

You'll always have a place here, Sister, Brother. That's what I tell them, and I open my weary arms. All traitors shall be forgiven. Come back anytime. We love you still.

The weather turns, as sudden as one of Jim's moods, and there's a part of me that wonders if he isn't to blame for the crashing rain, the sky whipping like a black sheet in the wind. An itty-bitty part, though I know he can't control the heavens, isn't even in control of what's going on down here.

I'll kill you! One of our sisters is screaming herself hoarse. Bring those kids back here! Don't take those kids!

Then she's rushing her husband from behind, tugging her little boy from his arms till it seems they're gonna tear him limb from limb, and it takes both our lawyers and two brothers from security to separate them. After all that, the whole family turn back to the pavilion together, soaked through and grumbling. I make my way over, my voice low and sure as I try to soothe some right back into this wrongness.

Shhh. How's about we take these babies to the TV room? I betcha they got some friends in there watching Willy Wonka.

The media flank the remaining deserters, all huddled under clear plastic ponchos, as they track through orange mud to the truck that'll take them back to the airstrip and, from there, the capital. My own boys, full-grown and strong as warriors, are in the capital now. I feel a prick of yearning that they could be here restoring order, and it's selfish. I feel a prick of relief that they're far from this mayhem, and that's selfish, too. I push all thoughts of them from my mind and focus on shushing, stroking.

You hear? one sister says to another. Congressman wants to stay overnight 'case there's more traitors.

Fucker's gotta death-wish.

Sisters, I cut in. Take these kids and their mama someplace quiet. Brother … we're real glad you decided to stay with us. Let's get you dried off, huh.

Jim slumps muddy-legged in the playground, watching them board the truck. One of his college girls, the favourite who stole his heart ten years ago and pumped it full of political ambitions, shields his head with an umbrella. If it weren't for her, he'd probably be crouched in the mud like a frog. So I guess that's something.

A dozen outta one thousand isn't nothing to feel bad about, I say, coming up beside them, though I know well enough that's not how he sees it.

Sixteen, Jim's favourite corrects, not looking at me.

The truck grumbles. Jim's second-favourite stands in the mud beside it, blouse drenched see-through, cussing out the passengers. I sigh to myself and head for cover under the swingset, managing a thin smile for the nearest brother from security.

Lord. This's some rain.

I never saw it like this, the brother says. Not in all the time I been here.

A shout sounds from the pavilion, and the gathering beneath its roof swells to one side. What the fuck? the brother mutters, breaking into a jog. A couple of newsmen leap down from the truck, cameras at the ready.

Jim turns slowly, mouth agape, one college girl at either side.

My hair's sticking to my face by the time I get in eyeshot. A pile of our brothers are holding down burly Brother Ujara, whose chest is heaving, eyes bull-mad and glazed. A little ways off, the congressman is rubbing at his Adam's apple, grumbling to the lawyers. I see the blood on his shirtfront.

Mother's comin'! one of our sisters hollers when she notices me bustling closer.

Make way for Mother Marceline!

Mother Marcie's here!

I'm within a foot of the congressman, close enough to see the little silver curls on his back, to smell the slick salt red of him. It hooks me the way the smell of blood has since nursing school, narrowing my field of vision and quieting the shouting to a hush.

Congressman, I coo. Let me take a look at that.

He flinches. Grimaces like I just suggested sticking my fingers right in his neck.

Nothing more than a razor nick, he says. A little arrogant, but then you'd have to be to come down here all guns blazing, quoting the constitution.

Mother's a damn fine nurse, assures Brother Tim, our head of security, as he escorts us out of the crowd.

On behalf of our entire community, I want to apologise, I go on. I hope you'll forgive folks for acting out of turn. Emotions are running high.

The rain is ricocheting off the aluminium roof, off our cheeks as we wade into it, college girls chasing behind us with another couple umbrellas. The lawyers are saying it wouldn't be wise for the congressman to stay in Jonestown tonight, not with the mood of hostility, and he's agreeing, fumbling with his shirt buttons, and I'm agreeing, too. My husband is coming to meet us with that same half-dead expression, and I don't know if it's just the muddle of his mind these days, but I wish he'd look more surprised.

Jim holds out his hand. Does this change things?

It changes some things, the congressman says, shaking Jim's hand just the same.

And of course every one of us knows it's true. Once blood is spilled, no matter how little, things are bound to get a whole lot more serious.

EVERYONE. PLEASE RETURN TO YOUR COTTAGES TO REST. I REPEAT, PLEASE RETURN TO YOUR COTTAGES TO REST.

The echo of my voice over the PA makes me prickle with its own thin jaggedness. Not a voice to soothe any more than the voices of the college girls muttering under their breath as they tap out Morse code to our people in the States. It's coming on dusk here; midday in San Francisco.

Did you get a hold of the boys in the capital? I ask Jim's favourite, the dark-auburn bun at the back of her head.

We spoke to Sister Sharon, she says with a lemon-suck of her lips. They've been given the order for retaliation.

Then she gets right back to fiddling with the radio.

I turn away, stifle the sob in my chest like a yawn during one of Jim's all-night sermons. Could my boys kill? It's something we've whispered about when their father is at his sickest; what it means to keep this community alive, to protect it from threats outside and in. I've seen the rage in my boys, their potential for mutiny, and how it's always stopped just short of strangling Jim in his sleep. To kill a sick man would be too easy for our kind, so used to doing things the hard way, to weathering the sickest storms.

To kill on a sick man's orders? Well. I hope not.

Jim's second-favourite slams in, her dark eyes huge and with more rings than Saturn. So skinny it's hard to believe that wild wind didn't blow her in.

Father wants everyone back at the pavilion, she declares.

Lord, I sigh. It's like musical chairs here.

There's no time for rest, she says. She sticks out her chin, looking almost pleased with herself for knowing what I don't: Some of the brothers from security took the guns and went after the congressman's party.

Oh. Good Lord. I close my eyes. When I open them she's looking at me like I'm foolish to use the Lord's name, even in vain. I look away and go to the mic before any of those girls can.

EVERYONE. PLEASE REPORT TO THE PAVILION. I REPEAT, PLEASE REPORT TO THE PAVILION.

Jim's favourite hunches into her headphones, spine lizard-bumped, not looking at all like a woman who's borne him a child, though she has. His second-favourite tinkles the chain of keys around her neck, wrests open a filing cabinet, her elbows baubled with bones thicker than the arms above them. These are the women my husband likes best: thin, and tireless, and scornful of all other gods.

I push outside.

The rain has stopped, but the wind is still screaming and thrashing the fronds of our palms and plantains. Toward the heart of the pavilion, our people course, young brothers sprinting ahead, sisters trailing with the kids, old folks bringing up the rear.

We're gonna commit revolutionary suicide! a brother booms, face dark and wet as he grins over his shoulder at a group of sisters. All brightly-dressed, long-necked, heavy-lidded, hair in cornrows or naturals or bandanas.

Except for a blink, maybe an eye-roll, they don't react.

The past and future are burning sunrise and sunset, and the day between them keeps getting smaller. It's swallowed up in shadow. THOSE WHO DO NOT REMEMBER THE PAST ARE CONDEMNED TO REPEAT IT, reads the black-and-white sign above my husband's head, the same that hung over the congressman when he stood up and praised us not 24 hours ago.

The congrethman's DEAD, Jim slurs into the mic, and he looks so slack, so heavy, rolling his shiny black-haired head. Pleaaathe get us some medication. It'th thimple … No convulsions … Get movin', get movin', before it'th too late …

I remember the past, for what it's worth. That year of going steady, when he was just a moon-faced slum kid working nights as an orderly, unafraid to speak up about the injustices he saw, the failings of the church and government. That first year of marriage, how he so hated seeing me pray he threatened to throw himself out the window of our Indianapolis apartment. Those first infidelities in California, how he alternately wept and grinned telling me of those liberated college girls, ready to slit their wrists if they couldn't have him. The first time I tried to take the boys and leave him, how easily he blocked my path: told me he'd sooner have us all dead than not by his side.

I remember the past, but that doesn't keep the same old patterns from repeating.

Our Dr Larry, who delivered all those beautiful babies now bundled at their mothers' breasts, oversees the other nurses at the wooden table as they squeeze purple liquid into the plastic syringes. All that's left of this day is a damp, moonish glow beyond the pavilion. The mothers are looking around with thousand-year-old eyes, looking as I do at the jungle and all its lurking violence. That congressman dead on the airstrip. Traitors and newsmen, dead. Authorities ready to storm our dorms, our schoolhouse, our nursery. America, coming back to claim us with a vengeance.

Don't be afraid to die! If theeth people land out here, they'll torture our children! They'll torture our theniors! We cannot have thithh! Jim's voice, sputtery and drug-muddled as it is, still has some of that old music that first got me listening. Are you gonna theparate yourthelf from whoever shot the congrethman?

Hell no! our people cry.

No, no, no, no!

That big metal vat with the purple drink inside is almost close enough for me to reach and touch. The leg of the table, to tap with my sandal. Someone elbows me, Sister Kathy sterilising a hypodermic needle, her cropped hair stringy with perspiration. She looks at me, apologetic. Surely as the night is coming I should be doing something. Something other than getting underfoot. Standing by him, assuring our people what's best, to leave this life of suffering together before they tear our babies from our arms.

I drift around the front of the stage, my body moving tall, pale, and weary. It will be a blessing to cast this body aside, its private aches and indignities. It will be a blessing to be among those shiny faces, smiles twitching at their cheeks.

I'm ready, Father, a young sister whispers, sweet and hoarse, touching her heart.

A hurrah rips through the pavilion as the brothers from security drive back in, jump off the tractor, and swagger over, guns high above their heads. Our toughest young men from the ghettoes of Watts, East Oakland, the Fillmore. They disperse to the edge of the pavilion and the crowd gets tighter, a few whimpers rising up from the back, a smothering of whoops and applause. I think again of my boys in the capital, the killing they're supposed to be doing, and the sting in my throat says: *no, no more.*

We kilt the congressman! an older sister calls out. We kilt him an' I'm GLAD he's DEAD!

It's his fault! cries another sister. He did it himself, comin' where he ain't wanted!

An act of provocation ... Jim agrees. We been provoked too much ...

Father, I appreciate you for everything! You are the only ... the only.

Jim? I murmur, coming up beside him. I don't mean to challenge him, only to put some quiet into the moment, maybe give us all pause to think.

Hurry up! another sister shouts, and she's aiming her words

at the table, the women herded closest to it hugging their babies. Our sweet, strong, beautiful babies.

Jim? I'm close enough now to smell the sweet heaviness of him.

Pleathe, pleathe. Can we hathen? Hathen with that medication? Jim leans against me like he would a crutch, tilting his head at the newest flutter of applause. Pleathe. I've tried. You know I've TRIED. You've got to move. Oh, hathen.

Jim, I say, right in his ear. Small ears. Neat black sideburns. Those small neatnesses, what are they worth now?

From over the table, Sister Tina calls, high and tinny: You've got to move. Everybody get in line and don't push and shove. There's nothing to worry about, so long as you keep calm and keep your children calm.

Jim.

His shoulder under my freckled hand feels soft, like something boiled, but getting to him is harder than anything. After all those meetings we've had on the subject, all the votes, all the suicide drills, all the times my voice has shrunk smaller in my throat, all the years of swallowing grief, why should he listen to me?

Jim. Please.

Our first sister in line is holding her baby out, her lovely young face taut and brave. Yellow blouse crocheted with little white daisies; surely her best blouse, as surely so many of us are dressed in our finest today. Her cloud of dark hair glows violet at the edges. She pinches that button nose.

Jim. Don't do this.

That little mouth that's only ever tasted mother's milk opens in a tight, angry O. The purple liquid shoots in. Others, not mothers, might mistake those few seconds before he wails for peace. But for us, the waiting is a clenched fist to our ovaries.

Peace at latht, Jim drawls. Free at latht. They tried to take our freedom, but we won't let 'em. We won't be enthlaved again.

Hell no!

No, no, no!

The sister accepts a paper cup of purple. She drinks of it deep, winces, rocks her squalling baby. To joyous cheers, she turns from the table and walks out to the darkening fields, her head high. The line inches forward, more mothers and babies.

Jim. No more.

Thirty-three born right here in Jonestown, and not one of them who's ever had to experience America's racism. My sob is tiny as a kitten's bell, but somehow it's enough to get people noticing: our mothers in line flinching, our security brothers closing in.

Jim. JIM.

For the first time in I don't know how long, he looks at me: through the shade of his glasses, from the sides of his eyes, and truth is, there's nothing going on behind them.

Mother, he croons. Mother, Mother, quietly, pleathe.

Veronica

Dear Kenneth,

You do not know me, but I would like to meet you. My name is Veronica Lynn Compton (née Barrera de Campero). I am a twenty-three-year-old actress, model, and playwright. I am currently writing a play entitled *The Mutilated Cutter*. The play is about a female serial killer who strangles women to death and inseminates their corpses. It is a Gothic tale with a feminist twist.

I have never met a serial killer before and was hoping you could help me with my characterisations. The Hillside Stranglers case is especially interesting to me, as I have lived in Los Angeles my whole life and am of a similar age to your victims. As a female writer, my goal is to transcend the traditional role of victim by inhabiting a strong 'masculine' persona.

Please write me back and let me know if I can visit you. If you like, I can send through a draft of *The Mutilated Cutter*, so you can read it before we meet. I think you will find it a subversive and, above all, stimulating experience!

Yours,
Veronica

~~~~~~~~~~

June 17, 1980

Dear Kenneth,

I have gone ahead and sent *The Mutilated Cutter*, since you haven't replied to my letter yet. I hope you don't think I'm too brazen. It is in my nature to be passionate about the things that interest me, and you interest me very much!

There's something I forgot to mention in my first letter: as well as authoring *The Mutilated Cutter*, I am going to play the role of my heroine onstage. Her name is Lucinda, and she is a raven-haired temptress with a voracious sexual appetite. She has been abused in the past but refuses to be a victim.

I have also enclosed some photographs from my portfolio. There are a few risqué ones that I think you will enjoy. I have been told that I resemble the exotic beauty Isabelle Adjani. I'll leave you to judge whether I'm suited to the role of Lucinda!

Yours,
Veronica

~~~~~~~~~~

June 25, 1980

Dear Kenneth,

Another week and no reply! Perhaps I am not your 'type'? It's true, I'm more voluptuous than your victims, but most males adore my full breasts, my son included! CJ is almost eight years old but still loves to nestle up to me and fondle me through my clothes — the sly cherub!

I wonder, is it because you weren't breastfed? I know from the newspapers that you were adopted. Oh, yes, I have been following the coverage of your case very closely. Still, your true self eludes me. Who is Kenneth Bianchi? What is in his heart?

I have felt deeply drawn to you, ever since I first saw you on the six o'clock news. Tears were running down your handsome face. You spoke of your guilt and Angelo's. It was the most moving thing I've ever seen in my life!

Bianchi. Whiteness. Innocence. What poetry there is in contradiction, the dark acts connected to your white name! I've seen Angelo on television too but feel nothing for him. He doesn't have your poetry, Kenneth, your deadly innocence.

Yours,
Veronica

June 30, 1980

Dear Kenneth,

I want you to know that I don't disapprove of what you do. Killing, I mean. It is a natural thing, and everything natural is beautiful. Everything natural is meant to be.

Will you feel more comfortable corresponding with me now? I hope so! I have such a strong attraction to you and your case that I know we are destined to meet.

Don't fight destiny, Kenneth. Don't fight what is natural. Giving in is so much sweeter.

I have seen pictures of your victims, posed naked on the hillsides. There is something both poetic and erotic about how frail and submissive they look in death. I've been trying to do a painting of Lauren, who looks especially beautiful curved on her back, with her hand dangling near her cunt. Did I tell you I'm a painter, too?

Most people don't understand how such things can be beautiful. As an artist, I do. I believe your victims did, too, in their last moments, when they saw how strong you were and made the decision to submit.

What is it like to have such strength, Ken? What is it like to hold someone's life in your hands and watch them submit? I would like to know, for the purposes of my art.

Yours,
Veronica

P.S. This is a sketch for my painting of Lauren. I've added some ligature marks for effect. Photography does not do your work justice!

~~~~~~~~~~~~~~~~~~

<div align="right">

July 7, 1980

</div>

Dear Ken,

Today the sun is shining on me, more brightly than it has in months! Do you know why? It's because your letter has arrived. It has arrived, with the sudden hot brilliance of a midsummer's day!

I am sitting at my desk in a little patch of sunlight, thoughts swirling faster than I can scribble them down. There is so much I want to say to you, Ken, that I don't know where to start! Perhaps I can say it better in verse …

> *Two lovers open up their veins*
> *Out flows the ink, blackly, a rain!*
> *To mark the sacred slip of white*
> *That soars, on Destiny's wings, across the sky*
> *From Him to Her, a cageless dove!*

The dove is a metaphor for your letter, which comes to me freely, though your body is caged. I don't believe in cages. My parakeet, Dalí, has flown free since the day I rescued him from the pet store. His droppings are truly a small price to pay for the joy of watching him in flight.

It is the same with you, Ken. You deserve to be free. Any harm that comes from you following your nature is inconsequential. What are a few girls, next to the beauty of a predator in motion? Mere droppings on the face of the earth!

Yet, as long as you are confined, you must write to me. Writing is self-expression. Self-expression frees the spirit. I can see already that you have the spirit of an artist, wild and unquenchable. Oh, Destiny! Do you hear that? It's my heart beating in rhythm with your heart.

Yours,
Veronica

~~~~~~~~~~

July 14, 1980

Dear Ken,

Thank you for another wondrous letter! I am very flattered that you enjoyed my verse. Finishing a play always depresses me, so I often turn to poetry for guidance. Perhaps you too could find solace in poetry.

Have you finished reading *The Mutilated Cutter* yet? I am very eager to know your opinion of it, but don't let me rush you! My play is very sensuous and should be savoured like a fine wine or an afternoon of lovemaking. How I adore those luxurious afternoons in bed — dropping everything to be brought to climax slowly, over and over again, until the sheets cling to my body like a second skin ...

In answer to your question: yes, I do have a telephone. The possibilities of phone communication hadn't occurred to me, perhaps because the written word is my natural medium. It may come as a surprise, but I'm actually a very shy person. Of course, for you, I'm willing to come out of my shell!

My number is XXX-XXXX. You may call me at any time of the day or night, except for weekends, which I spend with my son. During the week, CJ stays with my papi in Bel Air. My relationship with Papi has been tumultuous, and my heart aches constantly being apart from my boy. But I am certain that he enjoys a finer lifestyle than I presently can offer.

I am breathlessly awaiting your call.

Yours,
Veronica

~~~~~~~~~~~~~~~~

July 22, 1980

Kenny,

Never have I had such a stimulating conversation! I am still reliving it in my head, committing your words and sweet tones to memory. Of course, I've heard your voice before on television, but to have you speaking into my ear felt so intimate.

Our conversation was stimulating in more ways than one. I was too shy to tell you at the time, but when you recited those lines by Robert Frost, I had an orgasm. Oh, I am blushing as I write this! Did I hide it well? I may be an actress, but some feelings are impossible to conceal.

It is strange, because I don't even like Frost. Just imagine the effect you might have on me reading Shakespeare! Could you do me a favour and memorise Hamlet's soliloquy before we meet? Please? You must have heard it before; it's the one that begins 'to be or not to be' ... I think it is among the most beautiful things ever written, so to hear it in your voice would bring me great pleasure.

In exchange, I would like to do something nice for you. Hush, darling, no questions permitted! It's a surprise — and only if you do for me the thing I asked you.

One week until we meet!

Yours,
Veronica

~~~~~~~~~~~~~~~~~~

Ken,

It has just occurred to me, thinking about our meeting in three days' time (64½ hours, to be specific) that no one knows I've been corresponding with one of the infamous Hillside Stranglers. If you were free, I might fear for my life. Instead, it is my heart I fear for. How I wish only my life was at stake!

You are the beautiful, dark secret that occupies me when I

should be thinking innocent thoughts. I have CJ with me this weekend. After much argument, Papi let me borrow his credit card, and I spent a heavenly day showering my little prince with gifts — polos, madras shorts, the darlingest sailor suit. And some sexy things for myself, of course.

Tomorrow, I think I shall take him to Malibu.

I've been having beautiful fantasies of lying on the sand with you, Ken; tasting your salty lips and feeling your touch on my scalding flesh. Already you are so real to me. How can I possibly be in the same room as you without combusting?

Don't be surprised if the world goes up in flames before my visit on Tuesday.

Yours,
Veronica

P.S. I hope you have been reading your Shakespeare like a good boy — though, if you have been bad, I cannot hold it against you. I've been very bad, too.

July 30, 1980

Dearest Ken,

Everything about you is perfect beyond imagining. Your luscious dark hair, curling gracefully around the nape of your neck. That neck — such delicacy, such sinew and structure. What I wouldn't give to be your razor, so I could nick your faultless white skin and watch the warm crimson flowering!

Strangulation, I know, is a very erotic method — but have you ever thought about slitting throats?

I think it would be wonderfully sensuous to cut a girl's throat then bathe in her blood like the Countess Elizabeth Báthory. She only killed virgins, and would drain them of blood then bathe in it. She also kept barrels full of blood in her cellar, which she'd drink at the table instead of wine.

When you are free, we'll have our own house of horrors, with a cellar for storing bodies. There will be dozens of them, all young and beautiful, and after we've drained them of blood we can toast each other over their corpses. Then we'll each take a draught of the rich redness and our lips will meet, still sweet with the taste of innocence...

Can you tell I am in a vampiric mood, darling? You are to blame, with your beautiful neck and all your rousing talk about *Dracula*. You are very clever to have picked up on the connection between my Lucinda and the vampiress Lucy Westenra! But it doesn't surprise me that you are clever. I am only ever attracted to intelligent men.

Soon I will begin auditioning actors for *The Mutilated Cutter*. After your splendid performance as Hamlet, I would gladly cast you in the role of Francisco! I was so wet, my darling, I don't think they'll ever get my scent out of the visitors' chair! But I am so glad you liked my surprise.

As I write this letter, my musk hangs over me like a heavy, tropical storm cloud. Do you smell it, Ken? Give this paper a sniff, if you are unsure. There's a reason why the ink is running, my sexy strangler!

Thinking of you always.

Yours,
Veronica

~~~~~~~~~~~~~~~~~~~~~~~~~~~~~~~~~~~

August 4, 1980

My Dearest,

You know me so well, though it has only been a few weeks. Who but you could have thought of such a gift? I love it, darling!

Most men's sperm has a stale odour when it's dry, but yours is light and buttery, verging on sweet. Freshly spilled, it must smell delectable! My mouth is already watering at the thought …

What plushness! Ah, what luscious red!
To circle your blood-swollen head
And lick the subtle, knife-made slit
That runs across, oozing manly bliss!

Sweeter than nectar, that first drop of love
Melting like a snowflake on my tongue.

I would be eternally grateful if you would describe it for me. The length, the thickness, the curvature, the hue — everything. I have seen many members in my life, but none as beautiful as I imagine yours to be.

Do you want to know about my first? It belonged to a boy from my neighbourhood. I was twelve. He was seventeen. His father worked for MGM, and they lived in a beautiful white neo-colonial. After he got me high and drunk, he took me to Topanga in his black Mustang and wouldn't let me go until morning.

It was a painful experience, but I am glad for it, as I am for all my experiences. A woman must know pain, before she can experience pleasure in its full measure.

Yours,
Veronica

~~~~~~~~~~~~~~~~~~~~~~

August 10, 1980

Kenny,

I am so infinitely blessed to have a man like you in my life, who is not only strong and exciting but so much more … intelligent, sensitive, poetic.

You have not been appreciated by the women close to you. If I were your mother, I would not hesitate to provide you with an airtight alibi. If I were the mother of your child, I would not keep him from you. Anyone who has spoken to you should know that you would never harm an innocent child.

CJ knows about you. Not you, exactly, but he senses that there is somebody. I've told him not to breathe a word to Papi, who never approves of my choices, though who he would approve of, I honestly don't know. I started dating Papi's friends when I was fourteen: lawyers, agents, acting coaches, even a heavyweight champion. I married the son of one of Papi's friends at seventeen. None of them were ever good enough for me.

Or maybe I was never good enough for them?

If only you were free — Papi's approval wouldn't matter, and I know CJ would adore you. It is his eighth birthday later this month. Papi has agreed to let me plan the party, on the condition that I hold it at his place. I have great ambitions for the day. Rest assured, CJ will have the time of his short life!

Yours,
Veronica

~~~~~~~~~~~~~~~~~~~~~~

August 15, 1980

Darling,

There are days when I am seized by a love for you so violent, I feel the world cannot take it, and must unleash some violence of its own. Last night, I heard gunshots outside my trailer, sirens howling in the streets. When I picked up my morning paper, there was a story about a *Playboy* model who was raped and murdered by her ex-lover. Is this all our doing, Ken? Or is it our love merely a symptom of some greater insanity?

I must be satisfied with my dissatisfaction, all the more as the days get hotter. At this very moment, I'm sitting inside my sweltering trailer, writing with one hand and rubbing my clit with the other. Can you picture me, darling? The fan is beating at my back. The Santa Anas blow through my purple curtains, offering no relief. My dark hair tumbles around my shoulders and hot beads of perspiration shoot down my breasts. I am perpetually on the brink, yet nothing can bring me over, save the real thing …

They are saying that after murdering her, the killer had her corpse as well. Then he shot himself dead in a guilty rage. They say it is a tragedy for a beautiful young woman to die that way, but I can think of worse ways to go.

A bullet each, Ken. How about it?

Yours,
Veronica

August 21, 1980

My Darling,

Your poem was so beautiful, it brought tears to my eyes. How have you been hiding such gifts from me for so long? Of course, I was aware you were gifted, but if I'd known you could write like that, I would've asked for a love poem long ago!

One hundred years from now, people will be quoting 'Ode to Veronica', as we quote Shakespeare today. Our love will echo through the ages, even when our bodies are buried in the ground. I can see us already, lying in a single casket, our hair growing long in death. As your skin shrinks from your skull, I will kiss your death's head grimace and fuse my bones with yours.

I have been very busy with preparations for CJ's party. Today I bought some cellophane and crêpe paper — my plan is to fill the house with homemade flowers and butterflies. For his gift, I am working on a painting called 'The Jungle of Delight'. It features all his favourite animals in an exotic jungle and the figures of a man, woman, and child, all naked. Some may disagree, but I believe in teaching children that the body is a beautiful thing.

You have asked, so I am enclosing a photograph of CJ. He is very much my own, with his beautiful brown eyes and thick eyelashes, though he reminds me more of you every day! You are his spiritual father, I feel. He has your innocence, your passion for freedom.

In return, I would love to have a photograph of you, Ken. Not like the ones in the newspapers, but something just for my eyes. Could you do this for me? Perhaps you could write to your mother and ask her? Oh, it would please me so much …

Yours,
Veronica

~~~~~~~~~~

August 25, 1980

Kenny,

The party was a great success! CJ loved being the centre of attention, the little show-off! I won't be surprised if he grows up to share my passion for performing. Even Papi was full of praise! He spoke of extending my hours with CJ and buying us a villa near his school.

I didn't expect it, but now that the party is done, I have so much energy! I've barely slept all weekend, I'm in such a frenzy — writing, revising, practising my lines. Don't be mad, but I even paid a visit to your mother yesterday! It wasn't planned, but when I called her about those photographs, she was so happy to hear from a friend of yours that she invited me over.

We spoke for hours. She loves you very much, Ken, and really seemed to like me — better than your son's mother, whom she had no praise for. She served me espresso and cannoli, and we spent a long time going over pictures of you. She still thinks of you as a nice Catholic boy. I don't blame her. You were such a sweet-looking child, especially in your first communion suit.

I went to a Catholic school when I was very small. I can't say I remember much about it. My life has been so full of chaos that I have trouble recalling anything from before I was ten years old. I do remember my finishing school, how cruel the blue-eyed blondes were, calling me 'chihuahua', 'taco', all the typical names. It was not easy being a 'Barrera de Campero' in a place like Bel Air. The only other Mexicans I saw were the so-called 'help', and Papi did not like me speaking with them.

I tried to change your mother's mind about your alibi. Though she believes Angelo led you astray, she wouldn't consider it. I wish there was something more I could do to help. None of my successes truly feel like successes without you here to share them. Your freedom is my freedom. Your chains are my chains.

What do I have to do to bring you home to me? I will do anything, darling!

Yours,
Veronica

~~~~~~~~~~~~~~~~~~~

August 29, 1980

Dearest One,

As I write this, you are smiling at me from across the desk. How that smile warms me! I would like to take your face in my hands and kiss those glistening white teeth, every single one of them. Alas, I must be patient …

The Mutilated Cutter is the key. I see it now. Perhaps it was your freedom I was thinking of all along, subconsciously, when I wrote it all those months ago?

You have called my plot 'ingenious'. Really, darling, you are the genius to have inspired it! Lucinda is your perfect match, the woman you bring out in me when we are together. I see now that I must strive to become her, in life as well as on stage, if I am to be worthy.

Tell me how, darling. Tell me what I must do and where and to whom. You are my master and I am your loving apprentice. I am willing to submit to your every command.

How willing, you ask? Well, just look at the photograph I sent you. I suspect you've sneaked a peek already, you naughty boy! Come, my precious, you can do more than look.

The photograph was taken by a friend of mine from art school. As she was binding me to the chair, I imagined that it was you giving me the Strangler treatment, and also that I was you, standing outside my own body and stretching the rope across my neck. Few people understand the psychic intimacy between killer and victim as we do.

The ropes around my body symbolise that I am bound to you, as a ring binds a wife to her husband. I am bound to you, Ken, till death do us part — though whose death is your decision.

Yours,
Veronica

~~~~~~~~~~~~

September 9, 1980

Darling,

I am so worked up from our lesson today, I can hardly breathe! How ironic, when it is I who am learning to take breath!

I have been practicing knots like you told me. My desk is strewn with knotted bits of rope and fabric. Poor Dalí doesn't know what's going on! He flew over to inspect and is now treading carefully between the knots. Oh, he knows I'm plotting something!

I can see the headlines already, declaring your innocence. You will be surprised by how many people are willing to believe you're innocent, on the basis of your looks. You don't have the face of a killer, Ken. Not the way Angelo does.

I wonder what she will look like, our victim? Her face looms in my imagination, but I cannot picture any of the details — the colour of her eyes, the shape of her nose, her lips.

Your face is all I see.

Yours,
Veronica

~~~~~~~~~~~~~~~~~~~~~

September 18, 1980

Ken,

I am composing this from my room at the Shangri-La motel. Do you know that 'Shangri-La' is what the Tibetan Buddhists call paradise? I doubt there are roaches in paradise, but if I use my imagination, the glow of the lamp against the yellow walls is almost heavenly …

I have been dirty in this dirty little room. I couldn't help myself. Not when I think about what I am about to do, how much closer it will bring us. To have your strength; to hold a life in my hands and watch it slip away … Never in my wildest dreams did I think that it would go this far, when I first wrote to you!

You were so sweet and concerned on the phone today, but you mustn't worry! Yes, I am doing this for you, but also for my art. I know now that I cannot become a truly great writer until

I have experienced what you have experienced. You have helped me to see this.

Paradise is near, Ken. The bars of your cage are melting away like a mirage and I am standing naked before you. I am ready.

Yours,
Veronica

Cathy

I've always had small hands. The rest of me isn't very big either, but my hands are almost as small as a kid's, with spindly white fingers and nails like broken seashells. David likes this about me. That there's something that hasn't changed for all these years, even if my face has gotten harder and my lips thinner and my cunt slack from pushing. And he likes seeing me do things with my hands, too, things you wouldn't expect from looking at something so small and white.

He's holding my hand when I wake up in the maternity ward. Last time I saw him, when he showed up in our backyard on Boxing Day, I was seven months pregnant and the hubby was sizzling sausages and the in-laws were all giving us the stink-eye. The time before that, I was loading the car with groceries as the kids played silly buggers in the backseat. The time before that — well, it was so long ago, I can't see any reason to bring it up.

'Heard you had a boy,' David says.

I don't feel like talking about the new kid any more than I feel like talking about what having him did to me. The doctors call it 'uterine prolapse'. That's just stuck-up hospital-speak for things heading south. David has probably seen loads of women since we were together, but I bet none of them ever had their womb slip out of them, red and bulgy as a baboon in heat.

'What are you doin' here?' I ask, my voice still thick from the anaesthetic.

David wipes his nose, taps his feet, turns his head to watch a nurse pass in the hall. He always did have trouble staying still. His fingers lick at mine like flames. Old flames.

'Cath. My life's nothin' without ya.'

I know it's David's house as soon as I see it. The shittiest place on the street, it's got this peeling white paint-job and broken orange roof tiles. Weeds cracking out of the path to the front door and about a half-dozen car bodies in the driveway.

My lips are thin, but I'm wearing lippie. I'm still a walking dairy, but I've got on my best blouse, with the big gold buttons and scratchy lace collar. It's only four weeks since the new baby came, but Mack's been out of work so long, he was chuffed when I said I was going back to the typing pool this morning. It'll be dinnertime before he starts worrying.

As I get closer, these dogs start up, big ones by the sound of them. David's always had dogs. Even when his olds could barely afford to put food on the table, there'd be dogs licking their dirty dishes, sniffing in their rubbish. I step onto the porch and rattle the screen door, and they go berserk, pushing their long snouts against it and scratching with their claws. Then I hear David

swearing at them in the hallway. I see his outline in a white sin-
glet, and he's kicking the dogs out of the way and holding the
door open for me. His eyes go to my purse.

'Didn't bring much, did ya?'

David was a scrawny kid but stronger than he looked. I saw it
every time he climbed in and out of windows as I stood watch, or
broke into cars and fiddled with the wires. He could climb onto
any roof, squeeze into any space. He could blow shit up and get
any car started. People always said he was dumb because of his
emotional problems and the way he could never sit still, but I
knew just from watching him that his mind worked quicker than
anyone else's.

No one ever said my mind was quick, but they did say I was
too clever to waste my life with the likes of David Birnie. As
opposed to Mack, who — even though he was dumber than dog
shit — never broke the law.

The sun is lower on the wall than when David let me in. I've
got the sheets pulled up past my tits. He kneels across from me
in the buff, rolling us a ciggie. He looks so good to me, it's hard
to keep from staring at the little trail of hairs on his flat belly, his
sleepy, dangling dick.

'… 'Member that night at the drive-in? *Livin' Dead*?' The
paper sizzles as David runs his tongue across it. 'Still got the scar
from that bloody fence. Hang on.'

He puts the cig in his mouth and shows me the white shim-
mer between his ribs. I touch a finger to it. Bungled robbery. Our
last night together.

'This one's from when I was a truckie. Banged my knee on the loading dock. And this —' he lifts a bit of brown hair near the front of his head '— Barge in Bunbury. Drum fell on my head.'

His skin ripples over his chest bones as he gropes for the lighter. If he was anything like Mack, he'd be snoring by now. He catches the cig with a jump of flame.

'Had this panel van. Yellow.'

He looks thoughtful. I wait for more, but he just takes a drag then passes it to me. A moment later he rubs his hands together and jumps up from the bed to peer through the blinds. 'Fucken dead out there.'

I don't have to look at a clock to know what time of afternoon it is. The kids will be home from school in about an hour. Milo and milk arrowroot biscuits. Skippy and Ossie Ostrich.

'Dealer's s'posed to bring a coupla eight balls this arvo.' David flicks down the blind and flashes me a grin. 'We ever snort together?'

I shake my head.

'You'll love it. Keep us going all night.'

If anything can help us make up for lost time, I'm all for it. I take the smoke deep into my lungs. Then I run my hands over the space beside me. Funny thing, we never got to do it in a bed until today.

It only takes Mack two days to track me down. He comes in the evening, when the clouds are all red and the sun burning orange like a sucked cigarette. David answers the door.

'It's for you, Cath,' he shouts over the noise of the dogs and game-show buzzers.

Before I get to the screen door, I can see Mack's holding the new baby. It's a cheap trick. From the way he's gawking at the dogs, I bet he regrets it too. I stand next to David and Mack's face goes all saggy and wet-eyed.

'Caffy. Come home.'

I don't say anything. He says it again.

'You gotta come home, Caffy. You had your fun. We miss ya.'

Mack's got a lisp. I notice it most when he's snivelling. He bounces the baby a bit. The dogs keeps growling. It's funny it isn't even crying when Mack is.

'Come outside. We're all waitin'.'

He waves his fat arm and I see them sitting in the car, the whole mob in their dirty polos and green check school dresses. So bloody plain and freckle-faced I can't stand to look at them.

'We don't care what you've done. We love ya. I love ya …'

I won't say it doesn't feel good to be standing between two men and hearing that. Even if David prefers to keep his mouth shut. Mack wipes his face with his hand — the one with the stump for a middle finger. Mack was a carpenter before he did his back in and gained all that weight.

'You can't leave us for him, Caffy. He's no good for ya. He doesn't care what's good for ya. Never has —'

It's as much a shock to me as to Mack when I slam my hand on the screen door and start screaming at him through the checked wire: *you don't know what's good for me, rack off, get outta my life.* Unless you count childbirth, I don't reckon I've screamed so hard since the coppers tore me and David apart all those years ago, chucked us in separate cells. When I'm done yelling, my throat hurts and the baby's crying as much as Mack.

'Sorry, mate,' David tells him, friendly like on Boxing Day. 'The heart wants what the heart wants.'

I'm still fuming after David chains shut the front door and sits me back in front of the TV. He looks at my hand where I hit it against the screen, the palm bleeding, patterned with tiny squares. He gives it little kisses. He kisses my hot face, my eyelids, my neck, and it feels sweet.

That same night I tell David, married or not, I want to live under his name.

Since I've started staying up nights with David, I don't like the way the world looks during the day. Blue sky. Orange roofs. Green grass. Everything too big and too bright.

He's always up about six hours before me. Sometimes he steals a quick root without even bothering to wake me. One in the morning. One straight after work. Two before bed, at least. There are days when everything down there feels like sandpaper and my piss burns like acid, but at least I don't have to worry about getting pregnant anymore.

David tells me he wanks on his work breaks, too.

'If I don't, I wanna throw spanners, fight the other blokes. Y'know?'

I remember how he used to get when we couldn't meet up. He'd do stuff like dislocate his shoulder trying to get out of juvie or smash up the windows of my house. And that was before we were even *old* enough to be doing it.

I like to watch the soaps first thing in the day, those rich

Yanks losing their memories and kissing their siblings. Sometimes I fall asleep on the couch after the soaps. One time, I nod off with a ciggie in my hand and wake to the carpet burning. David yells his head off when he sees it, but it's not long before we're lying in the ashes giggling like kids.

I hardly ever go with David when he walks the dogs in the evenings. The times I do, though, I see the way he checks out the women jogging and pushing prams, the bunch of uni students who live down the street and are always outside showing off. I see him looking at those students through the blinds in the bedroom, too. Without thinking about it, I get on my knees and start touching him until he rolls my head and groans, '*Shittt*, Cath.' And I know things will be sweet, as long as I'm giving him what he needs.

Every other Saturday night, David goes out without me. He showers and makes himself look spunky, with a collared shirt open to his chest and lots of body spray. He takes the coke with him.

I wait in front of the TV, smoking ciggie after ciggie and watching stupid prime-time movies. It's times like these I wonder if the years have changed him for the worse, gotten him too used to fucking around. I wonder about the kids, too: mine and Mack's, but also that one of David's they made me give up when I was sixteen, the ones that might've been. Then my eyes start to hurt, and the TV gets fuzzy. I doze off to newscasts and wake up to sci-fis or slashers from when we were young. Or to David.

'Shoulda seen me with this chick,' he shakes me awake to brag, stinking of sweat instead of cologne now. 'Two hours, no shittin' ya. She was cryin' by the end.'

If it's not that, it's voices in the hall that wake me. He takes them to the spare room on the other side of the house. If I'm in the mood, I get off the couch to see what he's picked up — always someone too young or too old, desperate and drunk or coked to the eyeballs.

One time, it's a blonde chick with a bloated belly. She's already passed out on the bed when I get to the doorway. He stands over her, dick in hand.

'What d'ya think?' He grins at me.

'She looks preggers.'

'Her tits are good, but.' David touches them. 'You like her tits?'

I climb onto the mattress. I circle her tits lightly. They feel like poached eggs gone cold, but the nipples are warm and firm.

'Yeah,' I say. 'They're alright.'

We start going out for drives on weeknights. Both of us miss the days of stealing cars. We don't say it, but the memories are there every time we go out in David's red Sigma. Doing eighty, we take Stirling Highway across the river, past the old factory buildings and flat ground that hasn't changed in twenty years. Dingo Flour Mill. Train tracks. Powerlines. Nothing growing but wild oats and bindi grass.

I drink rum and colas in the passenger seat and pass them to David at the lights. If I didn't know better, I'd almost believe no time has gone by since we last did this. But when I look in the mirror, there are lines around my eyes, and the music on the radio is different — sexy, jangly new stuff like The Bangles and Bananarama.

'Look at that one,' David says every time we see a young thing sticking her thumb out or waiting alone at a bus stop. 'Ask if she wants a lift.'

I do. Smile, wave, say hi in a cute way. I've got a squeaky little voice and am old enough to remind them of their mums. It's easy.

Once they've slid into the backseat, David does most of the talking.

'Orright back there? Not too cold? Wanna smoke?' His eyes flick to their faces in the rearview, narrow and bloodshot. 'How 'bout the radio? Loud enough? Like the song?'

He's got a trick of turning up the volume so the chicks have to lean forward to make themselves heard. Tits squeezed together. Faces just inches away. If they looked properly, they'd see him getting hard. But they don't even think of it.

David always has something to say once they're out of the car. Sometimes about their bodies, sometimes about what they're wearing, sometimes about what he'd like to do to them.

'Coulda driven to the bush and raped her, easy.' He smiles. 'I got a shovel in the boot.'

I know they're more than jokes, that it turns him on to talk like this. It turns me on, too, hearing how all those others are just garbage to him, how they can't touch this thing between us that goes back to when we were twelve and feels stronger than concrete. But it's not till he brings up his old panel van again that I get that it's more than just talk.

'Yellow van. Used to drive it around down south. Y'know, quiet places …'

'Lotsa space in the back. Fit a mattress, all my tools …'

'Picked up this one chick. Netball skirt. She was out late, askin' for it …'

'Easy as. No one found the cunt. Hid her good.'

I don't pay much attention to the old car parts David brings home from work. Mostly they just sit in the driveway getting rusty and keeping the place ugly. Even when he spends the weekend working on them, I'm not interested. I bring him sandwiches cut in triangles, and hang around to smell the chemicals and watch the muscles in his skinny arms as he pumps and polishes. Then I go back inside to smoke or sleep in front of the TV.

'Fixed up these tires,' he tells me one afternoon, coming into the bedroom and getting his grimy gear off. 'Can probably get a bit for them.'

I don't hear anything else about the tires for a couple of weeks. We keep going out for drives, making it seem more real by keeping a knife in the glove box. David wants me near the knife so I can keep it in mind, get used to the idea of holding it, of using it. It's up to me to let him know when I'm ready.

While he's chatting up the chicks, I open up the glove box and peek inside. I imagine grabbing the knife and turning around. But I always end up closing the box, and they keep getting where they need to go safely. After dropping off five of them in a row one night, David cracks the shits. 'Feel like a bloody taxi driver,' he spits.

I try to touch him, the way I did with those uni students outside the window, the way I've done so many nights just like this one. It doesn't happen though. It doesn't happen back at the house either, and David starts crying, slapping himself, bashing his head against the wall. He curls into a ball, his ribs and spine shaking, no different from that scrawny twelve-year-old boy.

The heart wants what the heart wants.

The next Monday, I'm woken at midday-movie time by David ringing from work.

'I did it, Cath,' he tells me from the other end. 'Found a chick. She came into work, right up to me. Wanted new tires for her Galant.'

His voice is rushed, happier than it's been in days.

'The other blokes were at lunch. No one saw. I told her to swing by the house after work, said I'd give her a good price.' He laughs. ''Member those ones I fixed?'

I nod. He can't see.

'You gotta do some things for me. Don't worry about the knife, I got that. But you gotta call her, set up a time. Got a pen?'

Pen. Notepad. He's drawn a cunt on the first page.

'I'll give ya her number.' David pauses. 'I told her you're my wife.'

There's a half-gram left over from last weekend, hidden in a drawer of the spare room. If David had plans for it, tough shit. I do a line on the kitchen bench before phoning the chick; another after hanging up. The rest I snort in secret while David's checking locks and fixing chains to the bed. When I'm done, I feel as strong as he needs me to be.

It's after six, and the sky is changing from orange to purple. She's got the right address. Still, she glances around after getting out of her car, like she hopes it'll be one of the other houses. Then she checks the number three on our letterbox, slings her bag over the shoulder, and starts walking up the path, ponytail swinging.

David flicks his finger off the blind. He takes hold of my arm. He's got the knife in his hand but isn't pointing it anywhere as he steers me out of the room, hard dick nudging me forward. When we get to the hallway, he turns me around and runs his hands up and down my body.

Somewhere out back, the dogs start barking.

'Go get her, Cath.'

I don't feel those steps to the front door, just my heart pumping hot blood. She stands in the shadows of the porch, clutching her purse. It's funny, but I can't help thinking how little she brought with her.

Karla

I'm sharing my room here with a nun. Seriously. Her name is Sister Constantine and she wears a rosary and everything, and spends all her time praying or else staring into space. The staring creeped me out till I realised she's just doped up, and now I totally want what she has. Like, why should some nun get to be high all the time and they have me on only 10mg of Valium, when I'm the most miserable woman in the country?

I told that to Dr Voigt yesterday, and he looked sad and asked if I couldn't think of anyone more miserable than me. I saw what he was getting at and said those girls' parents, I guess, even though I didn't mean it. Whatever they're going through, it can't be as bad as the crap I had to go through with Paul.

Five years of crap. The more I think about it, the more I think I must have been totally crazy.

That and under his spell.

But whatever spell Paul put me under is broken now. Ever since they printed his picture in the *Toronto Star* with those headlines spelling out exactly what he is. Because even though I've known these things longer than anyone, I didn't really *know* them. Like, I was always seeing them through the sparkly cloud of my love for him or whatever.

Now I know better. He's a loser.

A loser with perfect cheekbones, but that won't do him any good where he's going.

Sister Constantine wasn't too doped today and I was crazy bored so I came and sat on the edge of her bed. I had Bunky with me, and she smiled when she saw him and said what a beautiful bear. Bunky was one of the first gifts Paul ever gave me but that's not Bunky's fault and he *is* beautiful — plush and white with a velvety brown nose and real glass-button eyes. Even with all the bad associations, I'm never giving him up.

Anyway, I was sitting next to Sister Constantine and she had out her Bible, an old black one that's frayed at the edges. I asked her what it's like to believe in that crap, and she said it's a trial sometimes but makes life worth living. Then I asked her about Hell.

Hell is eternal death, is what Sister Constantine told me. It's like all the agony you can imagine multiplied by infinity, with no hope of it ever stopping.

She told me this thing as well, some Bible quote: *Fear not those who kill the body but are powerless to kill the soul.*

Now I'm lying with my Walkman in, listening to Guns N' Roses, and I've had my Val — 10mg still, but intramuscular instead of pills. Dr Voigt is finally starting to believe me about my drug tolerance being way high, and those bimbo nurses, too. They got me to hike up my baby-doll for them and stuck the needle in my butt, a sweet little sting I barely even felt. Yeah, my pain tolerance is pretty high as well.

I was on 'sleep therapy' when I first got here. Three days of cottony soft nothing, not even dreams. Dr Voigt says the time for sleep is over, and 'spilling' has begun, but the Val is supposed to keep me feeling safe and thinking calm thoughts. So I'm turning over what the sister said, thinking how powerless Paul is over there in his cell, and I'm me here in this room, where everything is soft and white.

I was sitting in Dr Voigt's office today with Bunky, going over my wedding pictures. Paul and me climbing down the stairs of the church. Paul and me in the back of the white horse-drawn carriage. Paul and me smiling as we take our first dance. They're beautiful, even with all the badness. I look like a princess in my puffy white dress, and Paul is my prince, so blond, *so* handsome.

You look sad, Dr Voigt told me. Like you're at a funeral.

Everyone says I look pretty in those photographs so I was offended but whatever; the doctor is always right. Especially Dr Voigt, who's like a doctor in a movie with his beard and glasses and that accent.

You're right, I told him. I *do* look sad.

Dr Voigt wanted to know whose funeral I thought it was, and I said Leslie's, since she was killed so close to the wedding. I told a story about driving around the lake in our carriage, and feeling sick because Leslie's body had gone in a lake too.

But it was also your funeral, Dr Voigt suggested.

My funeral, because part of me died with Leslie, and because marrying Paul was like dying again for eternity. It was like Hell.

We talked more about Hell. 'My honeymoon from Hell', I called that week in Hawaii. Us driving around the island, and Paul seeing a girl he liked and wanting to take her back to the hotel. Us climbing some totally blah volcano, and Paul hitting me because I wasn't filming right, not getting the smoke in the background when he was standing in front of it. Then I filmed myself in secret back at the hotel saying how much I loved him, more than all the sand on the beach, more than the Hawaiian sunset, more than life itself.

Anyway, Dr Voigt says we're making progress and I cried a lot so they're going to give me lots of drugs — 30mg of Val at least, and hopefully some of that Sinequan stuff that just zonks you out. My mind is a hard place to be right now, I told Dr Voigt. I've got so many bad thoughts.

Lori and my parents came to visit today and Lori gave me this book, *The Battered Woman* by Lenore Walker. She thinks it'll help explain Paul and me and, from what I've read, I think so, too. Like this:

Middle- and upper-class women do not want to make their batterings public. They fear social embarrassment and harming their husbands' careers.

And this:

Batterers are often described by their victims as fun-loving little boys when they are not being coercive. They are playful, attentive, sensitive, exciting, and affectionate to their women.

How perfect Paul was when he wasn't being a bastard. How perfect we looked to everyone else. Lori gets it.

I'm lucky to have someone like Lori in my life. Even before what happened with Paul and Tammy, Lori was always my favourite sister.

Lori and Mom both talked to Dr Voigt alone for a while. Not Dad, since he thinks he's too macho to talk and said he had to get back to work. Anyway, the three of us were chatting afterward about what they told to Dr Voigt, and it seems like they were both just ragging on Dad, how lame and useless he's always been.

Sister Constantine was in the corner of the room the whole time, staring at the bunch of daffodils. Lori thinks it's pretty cool that I'm rooming with a nun, and said I should try to find out why she's crazy. Like, maybe she's seen the Devil or something.

Dr Voigt was asking about my dreams yesterday so I made up some freaky stuff. One dream I said was like the Guns N' Roses music video where the bride dies, but I was the bride and Paul had killed me. I didn't see Paul killing me, but I knew he had, and I was seeing myself from outside lying in the coffin. I was still in my wedding dress and had a mirror over one side of my face, just like the bride in the video.

Dr Voigt asked me what it reminded me of, and I thought for a while then said Tammy's funeral. Because she'd been wearing white and also because she had that big purple stain on her cheek that no one could figure out. Even with a load of makeup on, you could still see that stain. Everyone who was at the funeral kept saying what an ugly way it was for a pretty girl to go, choking on her own barf with one whole side of her face messed up. And they were totally right, even if they didn't know the half of it.

We talked for a long time about how pretty Tammy was, like a doll, and how every little sister is kind of like a doll to her big sisters. I cried so much Dr Voigt gave me some pills and a shot, this time in the little blue vein in my arm. I had to lean on Dr Voigt on my way back to my room, woozy with a cotton wool ball taped to the spot. It was a cool feeling, like being Sleeping Beauty after the spindle pricks her or being drunk and taken home by some guy.

Not Paul. Just some guy. I miss that feeling.

Now I'm thinking up other dreams to tell Dr Voigt. Maybe something in the hospital with Paul as an evil doctor, cutting me up with a scalpel or whatever. And another one where all the girls are ghosts or vampires coming to get me: Tammy with that stain on her face, and Leslie and Kristen with electrical-cord burns and popping eyes.

Sister Constantine gave me a crucifix. It's a little one of false gold on a false gold chain. I decided to swap the chain with the real gold chain from my heart locket; the one Paul gave me our first Christmas together. Engraved *For Eternity*.

Anyway, she gave me this crucifix and also a holy card of the Virgin Mary who doesn't look like a virgin *at all* by the way. Maybe it's those frumpy blue robes she wears or the thing covering her head, but to me she looks, like, thirty. Nothing like the virgins Paul was always drooling over.

Long hair.

Knee socks.

Plaid skirts flipped up.

What a load of crap.

I was talking to Dr Voigt about the virgin thing, how Paul always held that over me. How what he really wanted was a whore and a virgin at the same time, which nobody can live up to. I was sitting on the couch with my legs tucked under me and fingering my crucifix, and Dr Voigt asked me if I enjoy 'sexual relations'. It was such a weird thing coming from him in that accent and me in my pink baby-doll. I giggled for a full minute then told him, sure I do, I'm not a fucking nun.

Of course, not all that stuff I did with Paul, I added.

Some of that stuff I'd be glad never to do again.

Because he's not just kinky, he's *sick*.

Dr Voigt ended our meeting soon after that, and I was still in the mood for talking so I sat with Sister Constantine awhile. Sister Constantine knows I'm married and that my husband used to hit me. She feels sorry that I've had to go through so much at such a young age and says I'm just like the martyrs, Agnes who got her throat slit and some other chick who died on a wheel.

It's Easter weekend, and they've been handing out little chocolate eggs with our meds, and taping up pastel decorations. Sister Constantine has been praying more than usual, getting all hyped up about the Resurrection like it doesn't happen every damn year.

Because it's Easter and because my family is coming to visit, I decide to change my baby-doll for something festive. So I'm wearing white court shoes with a long floral dress and my

'Blossom hat' — big and straw and loaded with flowers, just like Blossom wears on the TV show.

I've got a whole spill prepared for Dr Voigt, too, about how hard Easter has been, exactly a year after we took Kristen and all. How I tried to make her last days less painful by pretending it was one long slumber party, with some kinky shit thrown in between the makeovers and pizza dinners. Being a friend to her, basically.

In those three days, I was probably a better friend to Kristen than any of my so-called 'friends for life' have been. It's crazy how shallow people can be, ditching you as soon as they realise you're not perfect.

I got to see another psychiatrist today. He's an old guy called Dr Brown and he likes me a lot. We talked forever about my work at the animal clinic, and he was totally impressed when I said about French poodles being a good breed for people with allergies. Because of their tight little curls, they don't shed so much hair and dander.

Dr Brown got me to do a bunch of written tests and at the end a Rorschach, which I've always wanted to do. It reminded me of playing Ouija at slumber parties, making up crap just for kicks. He held up the cards and I told him I saw a mask, a padlock, a skull, crushing boots. At the end of it all, he gave me 40mg of Val and some Sinequan.

More tests later this week, and when I was on the phone to my lawyer, he said he'd try to get me profiled by some big-shot forensic psychologist who's worked with all kinds of victims of trauma — cult people and one girl who lived in a box for seven years. He's way famous, so it will totally help in court to have him telling the ways Paul messed with my head.

They're calling it a 'sweetheart deal' on the outside, or that's what my lawyer says anyway. I don't see anything sweet about twelve years for falling under Paul's spell, especially when I've given him five of my best already. Sometimes, sitting here, I get thinking about how I'll never be younger or sexier than I am right now, and how my skin is already less smooth than it was five years ago, and what will it be in twelve? And it makes me so sad I swear I'd trade places with those girls in a second, blotchy and rotten as they are.

Last night standing in line for meds I found out one of the other patients gets Demerol. She's not anyone special either, just some tiny woman with a bad dye-job and a name no one's ever heard. So I told the nurses I want Demerol, too, and in my veins, no more of those useless Valium pills. I can't even sleep on Val, I told them, it does *nothing*, and if I didn't get the drugs I want, the way I want, they'd regret it. They didn't believe me, so I started hyperventilating and cry-screamed that I was having a nervous breakdown till they called Dr Voigt.

20mg, in my left butt-cheek. Awesome.

Anyway, I had to give Dr Voigt a reason today about why I was so upset so I said I'd been thinking about Tammy, how scared I am of my family hearing the whole truth at the trial. Even though they've always known something went wrong that night, they don't really *know*. So he said I should try writing a letter.

I'm writing them this thing now, and it's coming out easy, maybe because I've been reading *The Secret Diary of Laura Palmer.* Thinking how my life is just like Laura Palmer's, with all the shiny blonde outside perfection and the darkness inside. It's actually doing me really good to get all this stuff out. Anyway, this is what I've written:

Dear Mom, Dad, and Lori. This is the hardest letter I've ever had to write and you'll probably all hate me … Then a lot more about how Paul was obsessed with Tammy and made me swipe some stuff from the clinic to put her to sleep, and how we didn't expect her to get as sick as she did. I can't be bothered repeating it all, but basically it says I'm really, really sorry and they'll never hate me as much as I hate myself.

My hand is cramping like crazy now, but I guess that's a good thing. Dr Voigt says spilling is meant to be a painful process.

Dr Voigt put me back on sleep therapy after I sent the letter. Two whole days I was out of it, but I'm awake now, feeling like I've just been kissed by a prince. A real prince, not a psycho lying bastard like Paul.

Lori wrote a letter in response to mine. It was on my bedside when I woke up, with a bunch of white roses. I was really scared to read it at first, but I sat there hugging Bunky and felt the fear flowing out of me. Because Lori gets it. She says she hates what happened to Tammy, but it's Paul's fault not mine, and he's hurt our family enough without me blaming myself. Also that she's lucky to have a sister like me, and so was Tammy.

They all came to see me yesterday, and no one said anything

about the letter. It's like it never even happened. We all just hugged and then we sat on my bed eating caramels and going over what I should wear to the trial. Nothing too sexy, since it has to look good with my crucifix. Lori and Mom said juries love that kind of thing. Thanks, Constantine.

Wanda

We have had many miraculous years together Immanuel and I. We have been saints. We have been pioneers. We have built our own handcart and journeyed through this great land from one shining coast to the next. We have been to Nauvoo and the Sacred Grove and Sugar Creek. We have been to Independence Missouri where Adam did dwell in the morn of creation. We have been to babylons each more wicked than the next Boston Philadelphia New York City. We have sat in empty churches and I have played heavenly music to congregations of spirits and angels.

We have had many miraculous years and now is the year of our Lord 2002. We have built the camp of all camps in these mountains and it is higher than the others and hidden from the eyes of men. It took four weeks to complete the temporal preparations of scooping out the earth and fashioning branches for the lean-to but now we are prepared for the arrival of the chosen young lady. I do not yet know her name or her face but

Immanuel said my spirit will know her when I see her as the first of my heavenly sisters.

Immanuel said the Lord would clear the way for him to obtain my heavenly sister but I am praying for him all the same. Ever since he went forth last night in his dark garments I have been praying. Now it's light and he's been gone I don't know how many hours and I can feel the back of my neck getting sticky in the sun. My body thirsts but I must keep praying or my vision may come true. It was a terrible vision of sirens and big jumping flames and Immanuel was being taken away in the back of a police car. Satan's voice was loud in my ear and he was saying *I have found thee Wanda I shall destroy thee Wanda thou shalt suffer eternally.*

The Lord never calls me Wanda and neither does Immanuel only Satan in his many treacherous voices and I must not submit to them. I hold my breath and envision the Lord enclosing me in his protecting dome of light. Then I see the dome getting bigger to enclose Immanuel as well as myself and he is walking through the woods unharmed with my heavenly sister. I cannot see her face in my vision but I see Immanuel smiling and then I hear his voice miraculously through the trees.

'Heph-zi-bah!' he calls me.

'Im-man-u-el!' I jump to my feet and call back to him.

There's the quietness of tarps rippling behind me and some leaves rustling and Immanuel's name going through my body. Immanuel was given his name in November of the year 2000 when it was declared that he would hold the keys to the Lord's kingdom. Immanuel says the keys are an invisible but constant burden which is why I must carry more earthly burdens than he does. Just last month we were provided with an abundance of food supplies from Albertsons and I carried everything heavy cans and a twenty-pound bag of rice five miles up the mountain in the burning sun. Immanuel carried only the keys to the Lord's kingdom and a carton of Heineken and he was ahead of me when I dropped to the ground on the edge of camp. Later I awoke and he told me I must have strength for my suffering was only of this earth.

We will not suffer in the Lord's kingdom not Immanuel nor myself nor any of my heavenly sisters. I am to have seven sisters all aged fourteen and chosen by the Lord and all to be obtained by force. We did not ask for it to be this way but so it was ordained and Immanuel the Lord's most faithful servant has obeyed. He had a rucksack with him last night when he went forth and in it some duct tape and bolt-cutters and the knife with the jagged blade though it has been foreseen that so much force will not be necessary.

I see bits of night between the leaves then miraculously Immanuel appears before me radiant in his dark clothing and holding my heavenly sister by the shoulder. She looks lovely young and golden-haired in silky red and I feel as I'm made of dust looking at her. Then her lovely face crumples and Immanuel pushes her forth into my arms and all of a sudden she's crying at my breast her slender body trembling.

I look at Immanuel to see if this is okay and his beautiful eyes hold mine. His eyes have always had a way of holding me ever since we met in Jolene Greene's therapy group. He held my hand too and listened carefully when I cried about my divorce and my children and the cancer in my womb. Though he was still called Brian and his face was shaved smooth even then he looked like an Immanuel. He looked like an Immanuel and it didn't matter that I was called Wanda.

Inside the tent is cool rippling blue like the stream below camp where we go to bathe and collect water. I haven't bathed this day but I have collected water in the big blue basin we found in the trash outside Shriners Hospital. The basin is at my heavenly sister's feet and she is seated above me on our best blue bucket crying again with her arms crossed over her chest. And between her cries she keeps saying 'no, no, no …' and pushing my hands away from the red silk pyjamas she's wearing. I have been very patient asking doesn't she want to get out of those torn clothes and wash off the dirt from the hike and what about looking clean for Immanuel? But at the last part she just yells 'NO!' so loud I'm worried Immanuel will hear from outside and I start to lose my patience. So I make my voice low and serious like I would when my children were disobedient and I tell her 'If you don't take those off by yourself Immanuel will have to come in and rip them.'

After that she listens starts unbuttoning her pyjama top very shakily and she isn't wearing a brassiere so I can see she's almost flat there. At her age I was almost a woman and all my daughters had womanly shapes when they were fourteen. LouRee especially would dress like a harlot in tight low-cut garments and was never obedient but one day I took those garments from her wardrobe and destroyed them. I think perhaps it is a good thing that my heavenly sister is not too womanly not wilful and disobedient like LouRee.

I help my heavenly sister remove her shirt from her shoulders. She does a small jump when I first touch her but then she is obedient. She holds her arms out and I am reminded of a doll how easy they are to dress and undress. Before Immanuel and I were commanded to destroy our earthly possessions I had many beautiful dolls all of them with faces of porcelain and hair golden like my heavenly sister's.

My heavenly sister keeps an arm over her chest as she takes off her pyjama bottoms. It pleases me that she is modest but I hope when the time comes she will let Immanuel see her. There is some bedding in the corner for after they are sealed and the sheets I washed just yesterday so they are very clean. She kicks the pyjama bottoms off near the basin then just sits there on her bucket shivering and not looking anywhere. When I tell her it's time to take off her underwear she starts crying all over again. 'No, no, please no ...' She holds onto herself tightly. 'Please, no. Don't make me. No.'

I try to make her hush telling her I need to bathe her and after she can get dressed again. I show her the robes I made just for her pure linen like mine and Immanuel's with long sleeves and a long hem. She won't listen she's too upset and for a moment I feel so sorry I want to tell her I know how it feels to suffer on this earth. The day Immanuel told me he had been commanded to take other wives I was suffering crying like she is and we were coming home from a wonderful Thanksgiving dinner at Chuck-A-Rama. It was only a few weeks after he was given the name Immanuel and I was so upset I called him Brian again. 'Woman, thou shalt not call me by that name!' he scorned me and would not let me touch him in any way until I called him Immanuel. After that he told me I must live by the word or suffer eternal consequences.

'If you don't take off your underwear, Immanuel will come in and do it,' I tell my heavenly sister. I don't tell her or you will suffer eternal consequences but try to make my eyes say as much.

She stops crying and looks up at me in a way like she wants to know if I'm serious. I guess she sees I am because right away she does as I say and I feel very righteous. She pulls the underwear down and stands up from the bucket bending a bit because the roof isn't as tall as her. Her arms are still in front to cover her chest but also her privates now too. I tell her to stand in the blue basin and put my hands on her shoulders. They are lovely shoulders white and smooth except for where the trees have scratched her. She shivers and I ask is the water too cold but she says no and this is lucky because I don't think Immanuel would want me taking more time to warm it. I bend down at her feet and get the sponge and start swishing it in the water. Then I'm smoothing the sponge up and down my heavenly sister's legs and they have scratches too and then between her legs and she sort of squirms. She only has a little bit of hair down there and it's very light and blonde. When I get the sponge up to the cuts on my heavenly sister's shoulders the water is dirty grey and she has goosebumps all over though she said she wasn't cold.

I tell my heavenly sister to step out of the basin and then I slip the robes over her head. She is glad for the covering and looks lovely I think and very clean. There's only one fault I can find with her and that's her hair being tied back so I tell her to let it loose. It falls down around her shoulders not as long as mine but silky and the gold colour is very beautiful. I touch her hair and say 'Don't you look nice now' and remember saying the same thing to my daughters when they were very young.

My heavenly sister gives me a little smile and her eyes are wet but lovely. I think maybe she wants to say something but I don't know what and anyway I feel suddenly cold knowing Immanuel is waiting. So I pick up the basin in my arms and see her red pyjamas all crumpled in the dirt and then I slip out of the tent without saying anything else.

Immanuel comes forth to meet me dressed in his robes. His face is glowing and he looks very handsome as handsome as the day we were sealed. He didn't have his robes then or his beard or the long hair to his shoulders just a suit and I had a beautiful dress sewed by my own hand. Our robes of course are more special than any garments as they were inspired by the Lord but still I feel prideful when I think of my wedding dress.

We have tried to wear our robes every day since Immanuel was called but sometimes like last night he has to take them off to wear dark clothes and also last fall after 9/11. During that time people kept refusing alms thinking we were Muslims so we were commanded to dress in street clothes for some months. Immanuel shaved his beard too and cut his hair and it was very strange to see him looking like Brian again but he impressed me to keep calling him Immanuel.

Immanuel's eyes are on me and he is standing so close our bodies would be touching if it wasn't for the big blue basin in my arms. The basin is full of grey-coloured water and I'm holding it low to my belly where my scar is. I've had the scar a long time since before Immanuel and even before Brian and it's very faded but I never forget it's there. When I bathe I always look down to see it and if there's sun it glitters beautifully as cobwebs and beer cans and other ugly things become beautiful in the sun. Immanuel says someday my womb will be opened up and I'll bear the next saviour which is why my scar is so beautiful in the sun. I wonder if the sun makes me beautiful now and I look deep into Immanuel's eyes and he speaks. 'Hast thou prepared her?'

I don't know how to answer Immanuel. If I tell him no he'll be angry at me for not preparing my heavenly sister as I was commanded but if I tell him yes he'll go inside the tent and join her right away. I don't say anything for a long time and Immanuel's eyes float from me to the tent and back. Then he takes a step to the side and quickly I grab onto his sleeve. Some water slips from the basin when I do this and wets his sandals a little bit and the dirt underneath. Immanuel looks at the dirt then at me and I'm very sorry.

'She has been bathed!' I cry out still holding onto his sleeve. 'She has been bathed but her spirit is not ready!'

'Didst thou instruct her to be obedient?'

'Yes I did I told her I did —'

Everything goes blurry and I can't see the look on Immanuel's face he's all blurred with the trees behind him and the heavens above. I think he must be angry though because he's not saying anything and suddenly I feel Satan's fury upon me. He's calling me Wanda again first quietly then louder like *wanda Wanda WANDA*. Then miraculously Immanuel's voice comes and disperses Satan's fury.

'Hephzibah, thou hath done good,' he says and very kindly he takes the basin from my hands and places it on the ground. 'The Lord thanks thee. He hath asked me to relieve thee of thy burdens.'

'A blessing?'

'Of a truth, Hephzibah.'

Even though I can't see Immanuel's face through my tears I can feel his eyes holding me as true as the Lord is with us in this clearing. So I go down on my knees and close my eyes and Immanuel puts his hands on my head. Right away my head becomes empty like a big basin to catch all his words.

'Hephzibah Eladah Isaiah, by the power of the holy Melchizedek priesthood, which I hold, I bestow on thee this blessing, that it may guide thee and comfort thee in thy turmoil—'

I am Hephzibah the most cherished angel favoured among women as Immanuel's wise and tender helpmeet. I am blessed with obedience that I may submit to Immanuel's righteous jurisdiction. I am blessed with strength that I may suffer without complaint and guard us against those who seek to imprison us. I am blessed in connection with my heavenly sister that I may live alongside her without envy. '— These are the blessings I seal upon thee in the name of the Lord Jesus Christ. Amen.'

When I open my eyes Immanuel is above me clothed in light and he's looking into the distance with his beautiful eyes. Then his hands leave my head and I hear the tarps flapping and look over and that's where he's looking. He sees me gazing at the tent and his face goes very serious for a moment. But forgivingly he says, 'Thou shalt rise now, Hephzibah,' and I rise from the ground with my knees very dusty.

After that Immanuel reaches into his robe and takes out the jagged knife he used to obtain my heavenly sister. 'Thou hath been chosen to guard us against the others,' he tells me very serious again. 'Dost thou understand?'

I nod my head. Immanuel hands me the knife and there's sun so it glitters very beautifully. Then he touches me lightly on the shoulder and brushes past and I turn just in time to see him ducking inside the tent. I look back at the knife feeling very righteous and listen to the blue rippling of the tarps and the green rustling leaves. In these quiet sounds I can hear the Lord's closeness and I am not alone I am filled with love. A moment later my heavenly sister screams.

APPENDIX

Blanche Caldwell (1911–1988) met Buck Barrow, a twice-divorced petty criminal, after running away from her abusive first marriage at the age of eighteen. He was arrested soon after, yet escaped from prison to marry Blanche in 1930. The couple honeymooned briefly before Barrow turned himself in and finished his sentence. They reunited in 1933 only to be drawn into a four-month crime spree by Barrow's brother and sister-in-law, the notorious Bonnie and Clyde. Barrow died of a head wound in police custody, while Blanche lost sight in one eye and served a six-year prison sentence. She remarried in 1940 and died of cancer at the age of seventy-seven.

Eva Braun (1912–1945) was seventeen when she met Adolf Hitler in Munich, while working as an assistant to the official photographer of the Nazi Party. They became lovers two years later, after the suicide of Hitler's niece and presumed mistress, Geli Raubal. For the next twelve years, Eva lived outside the public eye, shopping and vacationing her way through Hitler's takeover of Europe. She joined him and his inner circle in the Führerbunker during the Battle of Berlin in the spring 1945, marrying him in a civil ceremony on April 30. Forty hours later, they committed suicide together — he by gunshot, she by cyanide. Their corpses were immediately cremated by Hitler's staff.

Martha Seabrook Beck (1920–1951) was a divorced mother-of-two when she began corresponding with con artist Raymond Fernandez through a lonely-hearts club in 1947. Fernandez spent a short time at Martha's home in Milton, Florida, before jilting her and returning to his apartment in New York. Martha promptly abandoned her children and tracked him down, joining him in his lonely-hearts scams. Over the next two years, they swindled numerous women and murdered at least two others, as well as one victim's two-year-old daughter. They were apprehended in March 1949 and extradited to New York for a highly sensationalised trial. Both were sentenced to death by electric chair and executed in March of 1951.

Caril Ann Fugate (1943–) began dating Charles Starkweather, an eighteen-year-old local greaser, at the age of thirteen. Her mother and stepfather disapproved of the relationship, leading Starkweather to murder them, along with Caril's two-year-old sister, in their Lincoln, Nebraska home on January 21, 1958. Over the next eight days, Starkweather killed seven more people in a cross-country murder spree, taking Caril along for the ride. The pair were apprehended in Wyoming and Starkweather sentenced to death by electric chair. Caril received a life sentence and was paroled in 1976. She subsequently settled in Michigan.

Myra Hindley (1942–2002) was eighteen when she met Ian Brady, a twenty-three-year-old Glaswegian clerk, while working as a typist in Gorton, Manchester. They began dating after a year and soon began discussing 'the perfect crime', attempting it in July of 1963 with the murder of a sixteen-year-old local girl. Over the next two years, they murdered four more children, burying all but one of the bodies on Saddleworth Moor. They were convicted in 1966, both receiving life sentences. During her time in prison, Myra converted to Catholicism and applied for parole several times without success. After almost forty years of incarceration, she died of bronchial pneumonia. Brady continues to serve his sentence.

Susan 'Sadie' Atkins (1948–2009), Patricia 'Katie' Krenwinkel (1947–), and Leslie 'LuLu' Van Houten (1949–) were among the dozens of young people to join the 'Family' of ex-con guru Charles Manson between 1967 and 1969. The Family lived communally in various locations in and around Los Angeles, taking drugs, making music, orgying, stealing, and killing. Together with Manson and a male accomplice, Charles 'Tex' Watson, the three young women were charged with the Tate-LaBianca murders, a two-night massacre that claimed seven lives. All received life sentences. The full extent of the Family's crimes remains unknown.

Janice was fifteen when she began a relationship with Cameron Hooker, a nineteen-year-old lumber worker with a taste for BDSM. After faking a pregnancy, she became married to Hooker and he discontinued his sadistic practices until the truth was revealed, whereupon he declared he wanted a sex-slave. In 1977, they kidnapped a twenty-year-old hitchhiker, Colleen Stan, bringing her to their rented home in Red Bluff, California. Stan was held captive for seven years, spending the greater part of that time in a coffin-sized wooden box and undergoing daily torture. She was freed in 1984 after befriending Janice, and together the two women testified against Hooker. He received a sentence of 104 years and is eligible for parole in 2023. Janice received immunity in exchange for her testimony.

Marceline Baldwin (1927–1978) was a trainee nurse in Richmond, Indiana, when she met Jim Jones, a hospital orderly four years her junior. Drawn to Jones' concern for the less fortunate, she married him in 1949. Two years later, the atheistic Jones announced his intention to spread his socialistic ideals by infiltrating the church. Through a combination of faith-healing and social activism, Jones succeeded in establishing an interracial church, Peoples Temple, with Marceline acting as its maternal figurehead. During the '60s, the Joneses relocated to California, bringing their congregation and their large family of mostly adopted children with them. Peoples Temple boomed over the next decade, becoming a major political force in San Francisco. When allegations of abuse, fraud, and embezzlement arose, Peoples Temple relocated once again — this time, to the remote jungle settlement of Jonestown, Guyana. In November 1978, Congressman Leo Ryan led a delegation of media and concerned relatives to Jonestown. The visit resulted in the assassination of Ryan, along with several members of the media and Temple defectors. Over 900 Jonestown residents subsequently perished in an act of mass murder-suicide, Jones and Marceline among them.

Veronica Compton (1957–) was a twenty-three-year-old aspiring actress and writer when she contacted Kenneth Bianchi, a Los Angeles prisoner and one half of the 'Hillside Strangler' duo. They began a passionate correspondence, which led Veronica to attempt a copycat murder, with the intention of casting suspicion away from Bianchi. She was promptly arrested, and received a life sentence. During her imprisonment, Veronica attracted further media attention for an alleged relationship with another convicted murderer, 'Sunset Strip Killer' Douglas Clark. Veronica was released on parole in 2003.

Catherine Harrison (1951–) and David Birnie were twelve years old when they befriended one another as lonely, troubled children in Perth, Western Australia. By fourteen, they were in a sexual relationship and regularly in trouble with the law. After a brief imprisonment, Catherine was encouraged by a parole officer to end her relationship with Birnie. At twenty-one, she married Don McLachlan, the son of her employer. They had seven children together, including a baby boy who was struck and killed by a car. In 1985, Catherine abandoned her husband and children after Birnie tracked her down. She became his de facto wife, and together they resumed their life of crime, raping and murdering at least four women in 1986. They were apprehended when a fifth victim escaped from their house. In 2005, Birnie hung himself in prison. Catherine continues to serve a life sentence.

Karla Homolka (1970–) was seventeen when she met Paul Bernardo, a twenty-three-year-old accountant and serial rapist, on vacation in Toronto. They had sex within an hour of meeting and began dating, with Bernardo regularly visiting Karla's family home in St Catharines, Ontario. In 1990, the pair became engaged and Karla became firmly ensconced in Bernardo's criminal career, helping him to drug and rape her younger sister, Tammy, using anaesthetic obtained through her job as a veterinary assistant. When Tammy died from complications of the drugging, they successfully covered up their crime. Over the next two years, the couple abducted and murdered two other girls and raped several others, capturing their exploits on tape. After a brutal beating from Bernardo, Karla made a deal with the authorities that resulted in his life imprisonment and a reduced sentence for herself. The degree of Karla's involvement was not revealed until video evidence was recovered and her immunity secured. Released from prison in 2005, Karla was last reported to be living in Guadalupe with her second husband and three children.

Wanda Barzee (1946–) was forty when she met Brian David Mitchell, thirty-two, in a therapy group for divorced Latter-Day Saints. They began their rocky marriage soon afterward. Over the years, the pair's religious beliefs became increasingly sectional and they began preaching on the streets of Salt Lake City. In 2002, Mitchell authored *The Book of Immanuel David Isaiah*, a series of 'divinely inspired' revelations that named him as a messiah and instructed him to take seven young wives. Later that year, they kidnapped fourteen-year-old Elizabeth Smart. She was held captive and sexually abused for nine months before the pair's apprehension in March 2003. Mitchell received two life sentences. Wanda is currently serving a prison term of fifteen years.

BIBLIOGRAPHY

BOOKS:

Atkins, Susan and Bob Slosser. *Child of Satan, Child of God.* Menelorelin Dorenay's Publishing. 2012.

Barrow, Blanche Caldwell and John Neal Phillips (ed.). *My Life with Bonnie and Clyde.* University of Oklahoma Press. 2012.

Battisti, Linda and John Stevens Berry. *The Twelfth Victim: the Innocence of Caril Fugate in the Starkweather Murder Rampage.* Addicus Books. 2014.

Brady, Ian and Colin Wilson (intro). *The Gates of Janus: An Analysis of Serial Murder by England's Most Hated Criminal.* Feral House. 2001.

Crosbie, Lynn. *Paul's Cause.* Insomniac Press. 1997.

Fondakowski, Leigh. *Stories From Jonestown.* University of Minnesota Press. 2013.

Furio, Jennifer. *Letters from Prison: Voices of Women Murderers.* Algora Publishing. 2001.

Görtemaker, Heike B. *Eva Braun: Life with Hitler*. Penguin. 2012.

Guinn, Jeff. *Go Down Together: the True, Untold Story of Bonnie and Clyde*. Simon & Schuster. 2010.

Gun, Nerin E. *Eva Braun: Hitler's Mistress*. Bantam Books. 1969.

Jaffe, Harold. *Jesus Coyote*. Raw Dog Screaming Press. 2008.

Lambert, Angela. *The Lost Life of Eva Braun*. Arrow. 2007.

Layton, Deborah. *Seductive Poison: A Jonestown Survivor's Story of Life and Death in the Peoples Temple*. Anchor. 1999.

Lee, Carol Ann. *One of Your Own: the Life and Death of Myra Hindley*. Mainstream Publishing. 2011.

McGuire, Christine and Carla Norton. *Perfect Victim: The True Story of 'The Girl in the Box'*. Dell. 1989.

Moore, Rebecca. *The Jonestown Letters: Correspondence of the Moore Family 1970–1985*. The Edwin Mellen Press. 1986.

O'Brien, Darcy. *The Hillside Stranglers*. Running Press. 2003.

Pron, Nick. *Lethal Marriage: The Unspeakable Crimes of Paul Bernardo and Karla Homolka*. Ballantine Books. 1996.

Reiterman, Tim. *Raven: The Untold Story of the Rev. Jim Jones and His People*. Tarcher. 2008.

Sanders, Ed. *The Family*. Da Capo Press. 2002.

Stan, Colleen and Jim B. Green (ed.). *Colleen Stan: The Simple Gifts of Life: Dubbed by the Media 'The Girl in the Box' and 'The Sex Slave'*. iUniverse. 2009.

Smart, Elizabeth and Chris Stewart. *My Story*. St. Martin's Press. 2013.

Smart, Tom and Lee Benson. *In Plain Sight: The Startling Truth Behind the Elizabeth Smart Investigation*. Chicago Review Press. 2006.

Vronsky, Peter. *Female Serial Killers: How and Why Women Become Murders*. Berkley Trade. 2007.

Williams, Stephen. *Invisible Darkness: The Horrifying Case of Paul Bernardo and Karla Homolka*. SDS Communications Corporation. 2013.

Wykes, Ruth. *Don't Ever Call Me Helpless*. Clan Destine Press. 2013.

FILM AND TELEVISION:

Helter Skelter. Tom Gries. 1976. CBS. Television film.

Jonestown: The Life and Death of Peoples Temple. Stanley Nelson. 2006. Firelight Media. Documentary film.

Manson. Robert Hendrickson and Laurence Merrick. 1973. Documentary film.

Murder in the Heartland. Robert Markowitz. 1993. ABC. Television miniseries.

The Girl in the Box. 2008. Ermmm TV. Documentary.

The Honeymoon Killers. Leonard Kastle. 1969. Cinerama Releasing Corporation. Film.

'The Killer Couple: David and Catherine Birnie'. *Australian Families of Crime*. 2010. Nine Network. Television documentary.

ONLINE SOURCES:

Alternative Considerations of Jonestown. The Jonestown Institute. San Diego State University Department of Religious Studies. http://jonestown.sdsu.edu.

Crime Library. truTV. Time Warner. www.crimelibrary.com/index.html.

Reavy, Pat. 'Wanda Barzee says she "learned to be submissive and obedient"'. *Deseret News.* 11/18/2010.

Reavy, Pat. '"He was a Great Deceiver," Wanda Barzee says of her Husband'. *Deseret News.* 11/19/2010.

ACKNOWLEDGEMENTS

The Wheeler Centre/Readings Foundation, for granting me a 2014 Hot Desk Fellowship, without which I may never have had the confidence and structure to move forward with this book.

Kat Muscat, for bringing me into the fold of *Voiceworks* EdComm back in 2012 and making me an infinitely better writer as a result. You are dearly loved and missed.

All the precocious kids I met through EdComm, who've been some of my first 'writer friends', and always encouraging, brilliant, and hilarious.

Rafael Ward, Ellen Coates, and Chloe Brien for giving feedback on many first drafts of these stories, and for being such smart cookies, generally.

Victoria Marini, my agent, for your unflagging interest in my writing career from the other side of the globe.

The team at Scribe, for making this book real, and especially my editor, Marika Webb-Pullman, for taking such care with these words.

Mum and Dad, for being the kinds of parents who listen to *Murder Ballads* and read James Ellroy, and who are unquestionably proud to have a daughter who writes about 'creepy' things.

Kathy, Maggie, Nadia, and Wida, for being your wonderful, weird selves and some of my favourite people in the world.

Pepsi Max, for being such a delicious source of caffeine. Iris, for being fluffy.

Finally, I don't know where I'd be without the love of a very good man, Kirill Kovalenko. You are all the birds, and more.